ARIS & PHILLIPS HISPANIC CLASSICS

SERGIO RAIMONDI

Selected Poems

Edited and translated by

Ben Bollig and **Mark Leech**

LIVERPOOL UNIVERSITY PRESS

First published 2023 by
Liverpool University Press
4 Cambridge Street
Liverpool
L69 7ZU

www.liverpooluniversitypress.co.uk

This paperback edition published 2025

British Library Cataloguing-in-Publication data
A British Library CIP record is available

ISBN 978-1-83764-444-5 (hardback)
ISBN 978-1-83624-548-3 (paperback)
eISBN 978-1-83764-458-2

Typeset by Tara Montane

Cover image by Ben Bollig in Bahía Blanca

CONTENTS

LITERATURA Y OTRAS CUESTIONES DE MENOR IMPORTANCIA / LITERATURE AND OTHER QUESTIONS OF LESSER IMPORTANCE

LOS ARTESANOS / THE ARTISANS

PARA UN ESTUDIO DE LA ECONOMÍA DE EXPORTACIÓN / TOWARDS A STUDY OF THE EXPORT ECONOMY

LEXIKÓN / LEXIKON

Contents

THANKS AND ACKNOWLEDGMENTS

Ben: I would like to thank Gustavo López for his brilliant insights on a visit to Bahía Blanca in 2019; Rich Rabone for classical guidance; Jens Andermann and Philip Derbyshire for sharing contextual knowledge; Eduardo Posada Carbó for inviting Sergio Raimondi to speak at the Latin American Centre, Oxford, in 2018; Jonathan Thacker for his help organising the Spanish sub-Faculty seminar at which Sergio spoke during the same visit; the University of Oxford and St Catherine's College for funding research trips to Argentina, including that visit to Bahía Blanca; Rachel Price and Carlos Fonseca Grigsby for their helpful comments on the introduction, as well as an anonymous reviewer for their insights and suggestions; and Sergio Raimondi himself, for his intellectual companionship and kind friendship over the years.

Mark: Thanks to Dr Florencia Nelli for patiently teaching me Spanish for many years.
Thanks to my parents and Kate for always insightful feedback.
The greatest thanks to Nicole, Freya, Gaby and Chris.

SERGIO RAIMONDI – AN INTRODUCTION

Sergio Raimondi's work is at once shaped by literary tradition and craft, and highly public and politicised. It engages in the most complex issues of his time, including globalisation, colonialism, industrialisation and degradation of the environment. All are rigorously analysed through the medium of the poet's art. His poetry may seem formidable at first because of the breadth of the allusions, the depth of research, the unsparing gaze, and the expert skill of the language.

Many of Raimondi's poems address what might seem unlikely subjects for poetry: industrial practices, global trade, or labour legislation. Yet there's also room for desert-dry humour, touches of self-deprecation and immense empathy for the individuals caught up in seemingly implacable historical processes. And at the same time the pieces are clearly marked as poetry by their visual shape, their syntactic alterations of everyday language, the measure of the lines, and changes in tone. It is this juxtaposition of the cold reality of the globalised world with the studied craft of the artist that gives his poetry its great power.

* * *

Sergio Raimondi (b. 1968) is a poet, academic, and cultural organiser from the city of Bahía Blanca, on the southern coast of Buenos Aires province in Argentina. Trained as a literary scholar, and active as a university lecturer, he has worked as a museum director and later Municipal Director of Culture in his native city. He has published collections of poetry and essays, and in 2007 received the prestigious Guggenheim Fellowship.

Raimondi's collection *Poesía civil* (*Civil Poetry*, 2001), from which the first group of poems in this selection comes, marks a watershed in Argentine verse, representing a culmination of the starkly realist or *objetivista* (objectivist) poetry of the 1990s, but also setting a new course for many writing in the 2000s. *Poesía civil* is eminently literary, with references to writers such as Shelley, Keats, Dante and the English metaphysical poets, in poems of long, rhythmic lines. Via engagements with writers as diverse as Antonio Gramsci, Bertolt Brecht and Paul Valèry, it explores the social status and role of poetry within a capitalist, commodifying society.

Poesía civil is also rooted in Raimondi's cultural and community work at the Museo del Puerto, an oral history centre in the industrial port-town of Ingeniero White, adjacent to Bahía Blanca. Raimondi's fashioning of what he calls, drawing on Brecht, an 'epic' form of poetry, capable of dealing with the most pressing issues of the day, interacts directly with the mission of the museum. Both address the connections between everyday life and the flows of capital and power through the region. The term also relates to the technique of his poetry, drawing on the classical tradition – particularly the epic – which Raimondi studied during his training as a literary scholar.

His latest project, initially entitled *Para un diccionario crítico de la lengua* (*Towards a Critical Dictionary of Language*), represented for the first time at length in English in the second part of this selection, is an encyclopaedic work that attempts to catalogue in poetry the political life of a society. Here Raimondi accentuates certain features of his earlier writing: a basis in detailed research; a distanced, even ironic voice; and utmost stylistic care, matched with a greater variety in layout and verse form. A selection was released in German in 2012; the full collection was published in Spanish as *Lexikón* in September 2022.

Raimondi in Context

Raimondi's writing is both international in scope and closely linked to his Bahía Blancan origins. Trained as a literary specialist, Raimondi has for many years taught at the Universidad Nacional del Sur, in Bahía Blanca, where he also studied. Bahía Blanca is an important city for poetry in Argentina. It was the home of the Instituto de Humanidades, or Institute of Humanities, founded as a centre for research into art and literature in 1956, and led by the humanist and poet Héctor Ciocchini, until its eventual closure after the military coup in 1976. The university has a strong humanist tradition, publishing the internationally recognised research periodical *Cuadernos del Sur*. The city is also home to VOX, for many years one of the most active and influential small presses specializing in poetry in the country. The *poetas mateístas*, or *mate*-drinker poets, a group including Raimondi, Marcelo Díaz and others, emerged in Bahía Blanca in the 1980s, and published graffiti poetry, murals, flyers and magazines.

Bahía Blanca is also dominated by industry, with ports, trading links to the north and the interior, and petrochemical plants. The sea front at Ingeniero White, one might say, is perhaps as unpoetic a location as one could find, yet is situated in a city that is alive with poetry writing and publishing. Bahía Blanca also has a reputation for political conservatism, embodied by the right-wing daily *La Nueva Provincia*. The city has a major naval base, with a strong military presence. It was also the scene of one of the most shocking incidents during the civil-military dictatorship, the so-called 'Night of the Pencils' in 1976, in which young activists – some still of school age – campaigning for student bus passes were 'disappeared' by state paramilitary forces. One of the victims was María Clara Ciocchini, daughter of the Director of the Instituto de Humanidades. These are all significant elements in the environment from which Raimondi's poems emerge.

In 1992, Raimondi joined the staff at the Museo del Puerto, and from 2000 to 2011 he was its director. Raimondi and colleagues worked at the Museum to collect the stories and artefacts of people living near the port, including an entire barber's shop donated by the poet Jorge Boccanera, who grew up locally. The Museum aims to demonstrate the ways in which the practices of everyday life exist in a tense and conflicted relationship with national and international politics. It collects and archives oral history and cultural forms not necessarily favoured by conventional museums, including local cooking. Another of the Bahían poets, Aldo Montecinos, has published collections of oral history and local recipes.

The critical texts that illustrate its exhibits have a certain iconoclastic humour. The sign by a large piling in the grounds of the property reads "In the history of Capital, construction is destruction." Another, accompanying a group of waving garden gnomes, reads "Salute your inner fascist dwarf." [1] The Museum is also an important centre for local cultural activities. It is staffed partly by volunteers, mostly retired women; it runs a market on Sundays; it plays host to musical events; and its afternoon teas, which restarted in September 2021 after a long break during the COVID-19 pandemic, attract many visitors and tourists.

Building on his work at the Museum, Raimondi joined the municipal government of Bahía Blanca as Director of Culture, a role directly responsible to elected political officials. In the first half of the 2010s he developed a packed schedule for the city, and one that reflected a broad and inclusive understanding of culture like that of the Museo del Puerto. Events included concerts, film series, mobile libraries, food festivals, cultural centres, military commemorations, historical museums, workshops of various types, and communication strategies using conventional and social media.

In his municipal role, Raimondi identified something like a continuation, or an expansion, of his poetic work. But with important differences: writing a line of verse, he stated, was not the same as writing an official form. "Perhaps in *Poesía civil* one can visualize a call for a type of State that didn't exist then," he wrote in *Revista Mancilla* in 2012 – one that is both politically and economically progressive and incorporates culture in the broadest sense of the term. Just as *Poesía civil* expands the range of possible poetic subjects, so too does Raimondi affirm, in the same interview, that in his role as a civil servant he had to see 'culture' in the widest sense and context possible: no cultural programme could consider itself apart from matters such as road building, house construction, or sanitation. Similar juxtapositions are found in the poems of *Poesía civil*.

In 2014, in response to political machinations in the government of Bahía Blanca, Raimondi resigned his post as Municipal Director of Culture. In perhaps his most extensive autobiographical statement,

---

1 All prose translations are by Ben.

he posted a long piece on his Facebook page (2014), entitled 'Hacer política cultural es hacer política' ['Doing cultural politics/ Making cultural policy is also doing politics']. This is part account of the projects that had taken place under his directorship, and part celebration of the work of his many collaborators. The text gives a striking sense of the breadth of cultural activities that took place on Raimondi's watch. He went on to talk about his attitude to contemporary politics, and the difficulties for those who do not feel an affinity for the traditional parties (broadly: the liberal *Radicales*; the popular or populist *Peronistas*) in Argentina:

> I don't have a classical political background, nor an organic relationship or membership in strict terms to any political party. I'm from a generation that's had a difficult relationship with politics: one that lived part of its teenage years under the dictatorship, got enthusiastic about the Alfonsín [*Radical*] Spring and experienced the disappointment of the governments of Menem [*Peronista*] and then the Alliance [centre-left/*Radical* coalition]. Perhaps because of that I'm one of those who could see in the current [Kirchnerist] government's project a recuperation and updating of the proposals and aims of the great Argentine democratic traditions. Two of those basic proposals are, without a doubt, the need to recuperate politics as a value and to make the State present in people's everyday lives once again.

The lack of a traditional party-political affiliation, and the air of disappointment with contemporary politics in the 1990s and early 2000s, are both present in *Poesía civil*. His cultural work was an attempt to progress beyond that disappointment by working with the state. He added that Argentina was a society in which involvement in politics and working in the public sector were often viewed with suspicion ("desconfianza"). "Cultura es trabajo colectivo" ["Culture is collective work"], he concludes in the Facebook post, returning to a recurring theme in much of his poetry: that the solitary composition of verse is not enough. Since leaving his role as Director of Culture, Raimondi has returned to teaching at UNSur, to his work with the Museo del Puerto, and to writing.

Raimondi has won a number of prestigious awards – including from the Fundación Antorchas and a Guggenheim fellowship in 2007 – and widespread critical acclaim for his poetry, which has been translated into several languages, including two books into German. Raimondi is also an essayist, and has penned scholarly articles on Argentine and international thinkers, including the nineteenth-century liberal essayist Juan Bautista Alberdi, the writer, educationalist and president Domingo Faustino Sarmiento and the Hungarian Marxist György Lukács. Their ideas, discussed, debated, at times ironized, are present throughout Raimondi's poetry.

Argentine Poetry at the Turn of the Millennium

Despite its universal themes and international literary references, Raimondi's writing emerges from a very specific literary and political context: Argentina at the end of the twentieth century. Poetry writing and publishing has surged in Argentina since the 1990s in spite – or perhaps because – of economic and political crises. Young writers, innovative styles, independent publishers and new forms of circulation have all emerged. Whereas in the 1980s there was a reaction against 'social', 'committed' or 'militant' writing, much recent Argentine poetry demonstrates a return of the political. Questions about the relationship between poetry and the state have been central to debates about the social role of poetry and poets in Argentina, and more widely in the region, since independence in the first decades of the nineteenth century.

Poetry in Argentina still has a political weight, in a way that perhaps seldom persists elsewhere. Examples include the human rights activism of poet Juan Gelman (1930–2014); poets' presence alongside senior politicians at international cultural events, such as the Frankfurt Book Fair; government policies during the Cristina Fernández administration (2007–2015) to promote poetry in schools; the role of poetry in first peoples' (in particular Mapuche) activism in the south, particularly with the publisher Espacio Hudson; or the important work of poets as activists and educators in prison literature workshops, like the Yonofui [I didn't do it] Project.

For much of the twentieth century, the relationship between poets, and especially politically engaged poets, and the state in Argentina has been problematic, at both ends of the political spectrum.[2] Raúl González Tuñón (1905–1974) began his career in Buenos Aires' avant-garde circles, but through his denunciations of political injustice at home and abroad, not least the repression of workers' movements, became an early example of the poet writing against the state. González Tuñón was an influential figure for subsequent generations of writers, including Juan Gelman and Francisco 'Paco' Urondo (1930–1976), who combined the exercise of literature with active membership of radical – and armed – opposition movements. There were, no doubt, many writers for whom poetry and politics were intimately linked. Yet, as Jorge Fondebrider (2008, 24–27) observes in his panorama of twentieth-century Argentine poetry, the characterization of poetry of the 1960s and 1970s in Argentina as largely political in its concerns – rather than aesthetic, psychological, or existential – is something of an oversimplification.

For Fondebrider, the 1980s were marked by a proliferation of often quite influential poetry reviews, not least among them Último Reino and *Xul*. This is the period in which the *neobarroco* emerges in Argentina, poetry marked by both the sensuous excess of its language, and a genealogy that went back to the Spanish Golden Age, and in particular the poet Luis de Góngora (1561–1627), via the Spanish Generation of 1927 (especially Federico García Lorca, 1899–1936), and the Cubans José Lezama Lima (1910–1976) and Severo Sarduy (1937–1993).

Fondebrider sketches the many debates, in the pages of *Xul*, Último Reino, and other periodicals, over the new poetry. With the return of democracy in 1983, there occurred what Néstor Perlongher, a key writer and theorist of the *neobarroco*, called "Argentina's secret poetry boom" (Perlongher, 1992). Soon, however, this boom would

---

2 Zaidenwerg (2014, 15) makes a similar point, favourably comparing state support for poetry in Mexico with the situation in Argentina. For more on the social role of poetry in Argentina, see Bollig (2016), in particular the introduction and Chapter 1.

be anything but secret. A key vehicle for this emergence was *Diario de Poesía*, a bimonthly broadsheet first published in 1986, which at its height sold more than 7,000 copies (Fondebrider 2008, 40). Despite its very varied content, and its frequently changing editorial staff, *Diario de Poesía* became closely associated with the appearance of a new literary current, *objetivismo*, or poetic objectivism, in Argentina.

Writers such as Martín Prieto (b. 1961) and Daniel García Helder (b. 1961), associated with the paper, were critical of the *neobarroco*. They wrote in and promoted a style that stripped away metaphoric and descriptive excesses, instead using colloquial language and quasi-cinematic techniques (close-ups, cuts, and establishing shots) to create poems that presented objects and sought, as far as possible, an objective point of view, devoid of personal impressions and sensations.[3] Raimondi, along with Martín Gambarotta, Prieto, and García Helder, was central to this tendency – as one of the *poetas mateístas* (see above), publishing in *Diario de Poesía* and other related magazines, working with VOX and other small presses and poetry groups in Bahía, and writing essays on the works of other contemporary poets.

There was a strong political element in these choices: this was stripped down, immediate poetry that responded to an era – the late 1980s and 1990s in Argentina – characterized by neoliberalism and executive excess, under President Menem – the era of 'pizza and champagne' in the presidential residence. At the same time, in his earliest poems, and especially *Poesía civil* – with his classical and Romantic allusions, and his attention to form – Raimondi goes beyond these debates, and the split between the *neobarroco* and *objetivismo*[4] This sets him apart both from recent tendencies in Argentina, and from the longer history of political poetry in Latin America. Nevertheless,

---

3   Prieto (1996, 29) sees one poem as the stellar centre of a constellation of writers, including Gambarotta, Daniel Durand, Alejandro Rubio, and Beatriz Vignoli, namely 'La zanjita' (1996), by Juan Desiderio.

4   For further details, see chapter two of Porrua (2011) and the chapters by Fondebrider, Genovese, Prieto and Dobry in Fondebrider (ed., 2006). For a synthetic sketch of the *objetivismo-neobarroco* controversy in English, see Ceresa (2015, 3–4).

those tendencies have left their mark on him in his combining of *neobarroco*'s interest in classical sources and care over language with *objetivismo*'s social immediacy.

As poet Ezequiel Zaidenwerg argues in the introduction to his anthology of recent Argentine poetry, *Penúltimos*, there are some surprising points of contact between writers who one might presume to be aesthetically and even ideologically distanced. Zaidenwerg highlights the linguistic work and literary references in the poetry of Washington Cucurto (pseudonym of Norberto Santiago Vega, b. 1973), a writer too often read in merely anthropological or ethnographic terms as the chronicler of recent Paraguayan, Bolivian and Caribbean migrants. Even Alejandro Rubio (b. 1967), widely regarded as the grave-digger of lyric poetry in Argentina, has a mastery of register and tone in his presentation of different voices through the monologues in his poems (Zaidenwerg 2014, 19–20). Such subtleties are certainly present, too, in Raimondi's work. Zaidenwerg argues convincingly for the need to take many of the poets of the 1990s from out of the objectivist or materialist drawer to which critics have neatly consigned them. And, rather than merely reflecting or reproducing political neoliberalism, the backdrop to much of this period, Zaidenwerg argues that poets have energetically called into question this political order (2014, 15–16). He goes on to suggest, by analogy, that just as the lyric did not die, neither did history 'end' – *pace* Francis Fukuyama – given the energetic resurgence of mass politics in Argentina, alongside the boom in poetry and poetry publishing in the 2000s. Raimondi would be foremost among such poets.

The critic Lucía di Leone examines the growing role of what she calls the *artista-gestor* (artist-manager), for example VOX's publisher Gustavo López, especially in the wake of the 2001 economic crisis. VOX was both a magazine (initially in print and later online – di Leone calls it a "revista-objeto" or magazine-object (111)) and a publisher, home to the works of Raimondi, Gambarotta, and many others. The project had its origins in the *poetas mateístas* (see above). This sense of poetry as community is also borne out in the anthology *Monstruos,* edited by Arturo Carrera, and published in 2001, in part a product of poetry workshops funded by the Fundación Antorchas, in which Raimondi took part, as just one of the collective artistic endeavours that have characterized his literary career.

From an economic point of view, publishing poetry is a disastrous idea even in poetically engaged Argentina. Many poets at least partly fund their own publications. There are few paying readers. Poets do not buy each other's work, as they expect to swap books. But here di Leone perceives something important: "the *demonetarization* of literature and poetry" (81, italics in original) – that is to say a certain degree of autonomy from the capitalist nexus, enabling a more effective critique of the contemporary system, precisely as we see in Raimondi's poetry.

In the introduction to their anthology (edited with Violeta Kesselman) *La tendencia materialista,* Mazzoni and Selci make an eye-catching claim about recent Argentine poetry, crystallizing arguments made by many of the poets and theorists associated with *Diario de Poesía* in the 1980s and beyond: that in the 1990s, and continuing into the 2000s with the work of Raimondi and others, there developed a 'materialist tendency'. That is, contemporary poetry was moving away from the linguistic experiments and pure sensuousness of the *neobarroco* in the 1980s, and the ethereal, spiritual focus of certain neoromantic tendencies, towards writing about people, places, and things. Furthermore, it did so in a way that was formally materialist. They sketch a poetic moment in which small and not-so-small reviews and magazines (from *18 whiskies* to *Diario de Poesía*), poetry workshops, art-spaces and other forms of collectives came together in frenetic and hyper-productive activity. This is the context in Bahía Blanca from which Raimondi's first collection emerges, with its reflections on contemporary politics, globalisation, and the role of poetry in their analysis and critique.

Civil Poetry

In the 1990s there was a strong tendency for the state to withdraw from the cultural life of Argentina, through privatizations, cuts, and closures, in favour of private enterprise and, in culture, mass media conglomerates. Written over the course of that decade, *Poesía civil*, a collection divided into sections under broad (and sometimes ironic) socioeconomic themes, was published at almost exactly the same moment – 2000/2001 – as the political and economic collapse that followed a decade or more of neoliberalism in Argentina. Alongside its quest to articulate the relations between the poet and the state, Raimondi's work also asks how to write poetry against a backdrop in which poetry seems ever less relevant.

Poesía civil was published by VOX in 2001. It is, from the very cover, a work of striking ambition. Its title, an echo of the Spanish socialist poet Rafael Alberti's collection, *El poeta en la calle: poesía civil* (1966; *The Poet in the Street: Civil Poetry*), as well as a nod to a phrase from the Italian poet and cineaste Pier Paolo Pasolini, suggests poetry engaged with the social and economic context in which it exists. Its many long, measured lines borrow the rhythms of the Latin hexameter, used in classical poetry for epic tales. As Martín Gambarotta observes, Raimondi's collection has echoes of the Roman poet and philosopher Lucretius's *De rerum natura* (cited in Ceresa 2011, 205), in both sound and scope: a study in poetry of the very nature of the world around us.

The cover image, meanwhile, is a Renaissance emblem or *empresa* (a kind of visual motto or lesson), a crab holding a butterfly, an image that earlier adorned the coins of Caesar Augustus, with the legend 'Festina lente', make haste slowly, or more haste less speed. This is also the meaning of the printer's mark – an anchor and a dolphin – of Venetian humanist and printer, Aldus Manutius. The Latin tag and the link with Caesar points towards Raimondi's interest in Latin poetry, as evidenced both by formal features of his work (particularly the intricacies of his syntax) and his translations of Catullus into modern River-Plate Spanish, under the title *Catulito* (1999). The multi-layered nature of the allusion also reflects the way his poetry draws attention to the often unseen connections between disparate ideas, objects and systems.

Before Raimondi's reuse, the image was found on a collection of essays from 1968 by Héctor Ciocchini, *Los trabajos de Anfión*; there is a poem dedicated to Ciocchini in *Poesía civil,* included in this selection, 'Héctor Ciocchini observa dos veces un mismo libro de estampas' ['Héctor Ciocchini Looks a Second Time at an Incunable']. The cover therefore displays in clear, visual form a dialectic between the revival of the classics in the modern age and the political demands made of writing, within the context of Bahía Blanca and beyond.

The first poem in the collection, 'Ante un ejemplar de *Defense of poetry* con el sello "Pacific Railway Library, B. Bca., no 815 (to be returned within 14 days)"' ['Before a copy of *Defense of Poetry* with a stamp, "Pacific Railway Library, Bahia Blanca, no. 815 (to be returned within 14 days)"'] defines the aesthetic and political aims of the entire book, as a consideration of poetry's position in the world. Several aspects of the poem's composition demonstrate Raimondi's prosodic care, which harks back to earlier sensibilities. He commonly uses hendecasyllabic lines, a measure cultivated by both *modernistas* and Spanish Golden Age poets. In addition, most lines have three stressed syllables.

The poem consists of two long sentences, each of which covers nine lines of the poem. The poem's syntactic structure shows a preference for subject-verb order, historically less common in Spanish than verb-subject. Instead it is resonant of English syntax, and in particular the work of the English Romantic poet Percy Bysshe Shelley (1792–1822). The poem distances itself from everyday speech, making language strange, while at the same time mobilizing formal and thematic elements of Shelley's source text, the *Defense of Poetry*. The distancing reflects what might be read as the fundamental proposition of Raimondi's poem: that the idealized and ideal poetry described by Shelley is removed from the day-to-day lives of readers by an unbridgeable gulf. Within this key poem of *Civil Poetry* therefore, Shelley's suggestions are considered mere ideology. The question of the relationship between verse and the daily lot of its readers is one that we see exercising Raimondi throughout his work. Poetry, as unacknowledged legislator of the world, to use Shelley's term, can instead become quite simply unacknowledged, which is to say, obsolete.

The paradox of Raimondi's poem is this: why does it criticise the utopian vision of the power of poetry proposed by a Romantic poet as an ivory-tower fantasy while at the same time being so very poetic? It illustrates how Raimondi and other poets in the 2000s strive to overcome the perceived split between a poetry committed to aesthetics and one committed to politics. This is even more striking as the echoes of the highly aestheticized turn-of-the-twentieth-century poetic style *modernismo*, and in particular works by the Nicaraguan poet Rubén Darío, bring together a view of poetry as critical of the instrumentalization of language in the modern industrial world and an attempt to describe, throughout the collection, that very world.[5] Raimondi's setting of Romanticism in a railway workers' library is incongruous, an incongruity only reinforced by the anachronism of reviving Romantic and *modernista* poetry and traditional forms in the modern age.

One of the main concerns of the first part of *Poesía civil* is precisely a questioning of Romanticism, as Hernán Pas argues (2007, 5) – and as we see in the poem 'Glosa a *Ode to a nightingale* de John Keats' ('Gloss on *Ode to a Nightingale* by John Keats'), among others. But there is more at stake than just challenging a genre or a literary movement; this questioning is fundamental to Raimondi's artistic project in relation to capital and geopolitics, from the foundation of Argentina as a nation to the present day. In an article on the work of Juan Bautista Alberdi, Raimondi quotes liberally from Shelley; this encounter between Shelley and Alberdi "opens up the possibility of interrogating the universal rule of literary concepts with the universal division of production as a determining perspective" (Raimondi 2010,

---

5 *Modernismo*, a late-nineteenth and early twentieth-century literary movement in Latin America and Spain that drew on near-contemporary aesthetic trends, including the poetry of Stéphane Mallarmé and Edgar Allan Poe, is not to be confused with Euro-American modernism, as found in the works of poets such as Ezra Pound and T. S. Eliot.

1). That is to say that the values proclaimed as universal by Shelley – in short, poetry as foremost of the arts – are in fact only possible within a particular context, namely a society with sufficient levels of development and technology to permit leisure, travel and the free exchange of ideas and cultural products. And while Shelley wants to separate poetry from the sphere of production, for Alberdi literature is, precisely, another manufactured good, to be valued on the global market just like meat or grain (Raimondi 2010, 3).

Raimondi sketches the division of labour proposed by Alberdi between countries that are literary-importers (for example Argentina) and those that are literary-producers (for example Great Britain). This division of course closely follows that between primary or extractive industrial countries and those with more advanced sectors, in particular industrial production. The latter countries include the England of the Romantic period, more or less contemporary with the Industrial Revolution, as Raimondi also points out in a subsequent poem, 'Poética y revolución industrial' ['Poetics and Industrial Revolution']: the historical result was parallel literary and economic inequality. We see this, too, in 'La naturaleza no es un banco' ['Nature is not a Bank'], while in 'Transport Costs', Raimondi addresses this in relation to questions of translation.

Raimondi argues that, beyond the proscription against aping literary styles inappropriate for a pre-civilized country such as the Provinces of the Río de la Plata at that time, according to Alberdi, "one must detect the possibility of thinking of the (economic, social, political, cultural, etc.) circumstances as defining values for what poetry is" (Raimondi 2010, 9). And at the same time, the striking argument by which Alberdi compares poetry to any other product – is a sonnet worth more than a barrel of fat, for example? – creates a set of incongruous images that are echoed in Raimondi's compositions.

In Raimondi's response to Shelley, this is inseparable from a book marked with the stamp of the Pacific Railway Library. The Pacific Railway, or Buenos Aires and Pacific Railway, owned the line from Buenos Aires to Bahía Blanca. It was part of a network that stretched across Argentina and as far as Chile (hence 'Pacific'), and one of the most important of a phalanx of British companies that owned the railways in Argentina from the Victorian era until nationalization under the populist president Juan Domingo Perón in the 1940s. Effectively, this was a form of economic imperialism whose cultural consequences include precisely the presence of Shelley in an Argentine workers' library. The companies were privatized and effectively dismantled as part of neoliberal policy under Menem in the 1990s.

The rail companies had been integral to the export industry that developed in the country and the port of Bahía Blanca. The readers of Shelley's work in the edition here were the agents, the 'legislators', not of an ideal world, but of the new American territory, via concessions, contracts and the ideology of free trade – as studied by Jennifer French, with her concept of a British "invisible empire" (2005) in the region; while the contemporary reader, the struggling poet, perhaps, is anything but that. Raimondi's work therefore forces the reader's attention towards the context and situation of aesthetics. It challenges the idealistic universalism of Shelley's poetics, for such claims disguise an unequal, even unjust reality. Poetry, in order to make a meaningful critique of the world as it is must confront and challenge such ideologies. We find a similar critique in 'Silenus at the Railway Station', where the local drunk stands in for the figure of classical sculpture.

The rebellion against Mammon (read: money, or, better said, capital) proposed by Shelley is based on changes, development, technologies and forms of communication that simply do not exist in other places. That rebellion also has its material bases in the colonization of other countries, in particular countries that export primary goods. The poet can only rebel against Mammon because of surplus value extracted elsewhere, the consequences of which for local people are referenced in 'Meditación sobre las estadísticas de embarque' ['Meditation on the Port Loading Statistics'].[6] At the same time, we are dealing with Shelley the revolutionary, Shelley the favourite poet of the Chartists,

---

6   This poem is included in the German bilingual edition of *Poesía civil* (*Poesía civil / Zivilpoesie*, ed. Timo Berger, Berlin: Reinecke and Voß, 2017, 80) but not in the original Argentine edition.

Shelley the strident critic of the repression of the worker, who is of interest and profit to the writer under conditions of neo-colonialism. The poem moves dialectically between Shelley's Romantic rebellion and its material bases, rethinking poetry for the modern writer in Argentina.

For Raimondi, the writing of poetry should therefore include the analysis of the conditions and effects, both historical and current, of colonization. The great ambition of *Poesía civil* is to analyse in verse not only modern industrial practices, the relationship between peripheral cultures and the centralizing or excluding power of capital, but also the capacity of poems themselves to carry out the analysis that is being proposed – as ruthlessly dissected in 'La literatura será sometida a investigación (Brecht, 1939)' ['Literature Will be Subjected to Investigation (Brecht, 1939)']: "debating literature / with criteria not designed by it." The poems respond, one might argue, to the German Marxist critic Theodor Adorno's insistence in *Aesthetic Theory* that modern works must show themselves to be "the equal of high industrialism," not simply to take it as a theme (2004, 42), in particular through their ability to analyze complex industrial processes and economic relations using sophisticated forms of verse, but turned to other purposes; such is the case in poems such as 'W' and 'Cracker 2 o Monimenta Ministri', the latter including the links between political repression and industrial development in the region.

The ambition of Raimondi's poetry is immediately apparent throughout the collection – at first reading, and even at first glance. Visually, on the page, with its large columns and regular blocks, we are faced with something that – in today's age of free verse – looks striking, daunting even. Even a reader with only limited Spanish will immediately notice the unusual syntax, with its very long sentences and syntactic inversions; others will see or pick up the echoes of Latin poetry.

A distinctive feature of these poems is that we have to learn *how* to read Raimondi – and that this repays our effort. Punctuation is minimal, and the reader has to carry the syntactical sense through the poem. This very particular composition sets up echoes and resonances of meaning, and is rhythmically satisfying, but requires some initial patience and adjustment. The poems work by obliging us to consider or imagine what it is that the speaker might actually know, something that we are almost never told. Many critics, including Marina Yuszczuk, have noted that irony is a recurring technique in *Poesía civil*. But irony in the strict sense, of saying one thing and meaning the opposite, is seldom present. Instead, in these poems much of what one might imagine they mean is not stated.

From simple statements of unarguable facts – many eggs produce birds (as in 'La dieta de Dante' ['Dante's Diet']), the 'W' factory is x meters big (with a passing mention of Union Carbide) – we as readers are left to consider why the voice in the poem might not mean exactly what it says. An aside or a turn of phrase may indicate the double meaning; in other cases, it is entirely up to the reader to detect the ambivalence, the only hints being the form of poem itself (verse as opposed to prose), and the para-textual presence of the material in a book by an Argentine poet, as opposed to the pages of *The Economist* or *Forbes*. These features, which make Raimondi's poetry at once so challenging and rewarding, are accentuated in his next collection.

Lexikon: **Towards a Critical Dictionary of the Language**

In 2007, Raimondi was awarded a John Simon Guggenheim Memorial Fellowship for a project then called *Para un diccionario crítico de la lengua* [*Towards a Critical Dictionary of the Language*]. The *para* – towards, or for – suggests both the ambition and scale of the work, and that it is a project always in progress, rather than ever completed. The collection was published in 2022 with the title *Lexikón* (*Lexikon*), and travels further afield than *Poesía civil/Civil Poetry* both within Argentina (to the north-eastern city of Colón, in Entre Ríos, for example) and abroad (the Liebig plant in Uruguay, China, Russia, Sweden and the Arctic) – as well as to the depths of the oceans and even into outer space.

Maristella Svampa offers a synoptic history of the years 2001–2013 that provides useful context for this collection, and with it some of the ways in which the poet reflects and questions his political moment. She argues that in 2002, with the combination of political collapse and economic crisis, new forms of mass politics displaced more traditional parties and movements – be it popular activism, *Kirchnerismo* (named after Néstor Kirchner, 1950–2010, president from 2003–2007) or new right-wing coalitions. She notes the rise of autonomous, grass-roots, often cross-class forms of political activism in the early 2000s. At the same time many small presses, independent publishers, poetry workshops, and other collective artistic efforts emerged in Argentina throughout the 1990s and early 2000s. Raimondi, with his cultural work in various forums and media, would exemplify this cultural moment.

The gradual emergence of the political movement *Kirchnerismo*, and with it what Svampa calls, critically, "progressive discourse 'from the top'" (160) brought with it heterodox economic policies and a repositioning of human rights and activist organizations, such as the Mothers of the Plaza de Mayo, under the wing of the state (160).[7] With its roots in Peronism, this popular (and, arguably, populist) political movement which has dominated Argentine politics since the 1940s is characterized, for Svampa, by anti-neoliberal rhetoric, a focus on human rights, and a Latin Americanist discourse (161–62). It also found favour with many writers and artists, in contrast to the longer Peronist tradition from which it emerges, with more funding and an expanded role for the state in arts and culture than had been seen for example during the Menem years, albeit against a backdrop of considerable economic difficulty. In the 2010s and 2020s, *Kirchnerismo* has alternated in power with right-liberal coalitions, including the government of Mauricio Macri (2015–2019).

Raimondi's cultural work is intimately linked to contemporary politics, and during this period he found himself forced to engage in what were often difficult negotiations with the local state apparatus.

---

7   The Madres de la Plaza de Mayo emerged in the 1970s, initially as a protest group again the crimes of the dictatorship, in particular the 'disappearance' of people, against which they protested with weekly demonstrations in the Plaza de Mayo (May Square) in downtown Buenos Aires from which they take their name. In subsequent years, with occasional splinterings and the emergence of related organisations, they have campaigned more broadly on human rights issues, although with post-dictatorship memory and justice at the heart of their activities.

His *Lexikón*, composed in part during this period, and often directly engaging with its conditions, studies the wider context: globalisation, the rise of China as a superpower, and Argentina's position as a player in a global game of extractivism, logistics, supply and demand. As the publisher Gustavo López once put it – hyperbolically, but with more than a grain of truth – the single most determining factor in Argentine politics in the 2000s was the price of soya. *Lexikón* aims precisely to explore such constellations in verse. This section outlines some of its most distinctive features.

Lexikón is an alphabetical sequence of poems, each dealing with a different aspect or theme from contemporary society. It includes poems on labour practices, technology, international relations, Romanticism, and literary and cultural theory. References to thinkers such as György Lukács, Antonio Gramsci, Michel Foucault, and artists and writers like J. M. W. Turner, William Blake and Keats mix with ones to figures from the history of Argentine industry.

For example, 'Panamax' deals with global shipping and the links between Chinese industry and Latin American politics (the title describes what was the maximum size of vessel that can pass through the Panama Canal, avoiding the costly circumnavigation of Cape Horn). The poem ends on a modern-day irony: where once stood the United States Army School of the Americas, infamous for its role in training repressive forces for dictatorships from across Latin America, where students studied their enemy reading Mao Tse-Tung, and whose graduates (including the former Argentine dictator General Leopoldo Galtieri) carried out atrocities throughout the continent, today stands a five-star hotel overlooking the main China–US trade route.

Titles in the *Lexikón* are given in their original language and alphabet/characters – English, Latin, German, Vietnamese, and many others – a decision made by Raimondi and one that we have chosen to respect; Raimondi suggested that the initial feeling of being disconcerted was important to the effect of the poems, with readers encountering words or phrases unknown to them, and discovering their meaning, connotations, and history over the course of the poem.

One noticeable difference from *Poesía civil* is the variation in versification: in contrast to the large blocks without stanza breaks of the earlier collection, *Lexikón* includes couplets, tercets, quatrains and other regular stanza forms, in a clear broadening of poetic resources. Lines, as in *Poesía civil*, tend to be of roughly even length in each poem, and the same metrical and sonic care is on display. This is even commented on in one poem, with its reflection on the relationship between the "efecto / rítmico ajustado entre sílabas, pausas y acentos" ["effect / of rhythm adjusted between syllables, pauses and accents"] and the port landscape being described. This is captured in the poem's rhythm in lines such as: "el movimiento de aquella grúa-portacontenedores" ["the movement of that container carrier crane"]. Here a poem that echoes the stresses of classical epic poetry, and especially the dactylic hexameter of the Latin poet Virgil's *Iliad,* describes the ever-changing industrial skyline, with the rhythm now echoing the movement of plant around the port.

One might read the poem 'Lukács, György' as an *ars poetica* or manifesto for the collection. The poem, it suggests, must be measured against both material circumstances and "las eternas leyes genéricas / derivadas de la crítica de la poesía más universal" ["the eternal generic laws / derived from criticism of the most universal poetry"]. It concludes:

> Esto no es expresión de una subjetividad exasperada.
> Esto es ámbito de una serie objetiva de exigencias
> desde donde recusar la segmentación cotidiana.
>
> This is not an exasperated subjectivity.
> It's the space of an objective set of conditions
> from which to refuse everyday segmentation.

If everyday life requires us to separate art and industry, this piece, like several poems in *Poesía civil*, urges us to consider them together. In a paper presented in 2009 and published in 2013, Raimondi reflects on Lukács' theoretical work on genres, and especially his writings on realism. The contemporary poet, Raimondi suggests, is almost automatically in opposition to (or perhaps excluded from) the market, because of the economic realities of publishing poetry. Yet at the same time, Raimondi argues, such isolation risks becoming a wider social ostracism, as the poet withdraws from "enormes zonas de la configuración de la sociedad" ["vast zones of how society is made up"] (2013, 14). The poet's "transcendental rejection" – that is to say, the literary aim of transcending the quotidian world – beginning in the late nineteenth century, could not, he argues, be divorced from the perception of occupying a threatened position in society.

Furthermore, the poet's withdrawal from the humdrum daily round represents one more compartmentalization of knowledge, another example of both the market's specializations, and the contemporary division of labour. "Hay que preocuparse cuando la literatura se vuelve una cuestión literaria" ["one should worry when literature becomes a [purely] literary question"] (2013, 16), Raimondi goes on to state. The solution is not to withdraw from the market, and with it from much of contemporary society, but rather to ensure that questions of economics, labour and production, are not absent from the poet's considerations.

Industrial processes and practices offer the focus for many poems in the collection. The poem 'Escalator' describes, rather in the fashion of the 'instructions' that the Argentine author Julio Cortázar humorously penned for many everyday actions, the movement of an escalator.[8] Its form is of seven tercets, including many fourteen-syllable alexandrines, and occasional rhyme, is a version of Dante's *terza rima*, a form that lent itself to onward movement and progression in the poet's journey through the underworld. The voice in the poem considers the way in which the escalator exhibits at once all the rigidity of metal and all the flexibility of a band. A banal point, it may seem. But this leads to a further consideration of "la relación entre el devenir de las sustancias / y el de las compañías" ["to what links the development of substances / and that of companies"]. For business, too, needs to be both rigid and flexible, steely and elastic. The poem ends on a simple

---

8   For example 'Manual de instrucciones' ['Instruction Manual'], included in *Historias de cronopios y de famas* (1962).

observation: the word 'THYSSENKRUPP' marked on the machine's steel. Thyssenkrupp, a German conglomerate, today most visible for its work in steel production, manufacturing and transport, was formed from the merger in 1999 of two of Germany's largest industrial companies. In the first half of the twentieth century, during the period of German imperial expansionism and especially during the Nazi era, both companies were integral to the production of arms. Alfred Krupp, head of the eponymous company in the 1940s, was later tried and convicted for crimes against humanity, including the use of slave labour in his factories.[9] This history of violence and exploitation is effectively erased by the modern, flexible multinational. The poem's form tacitly offers ironic comment on progress in industry, a leap forward that tries to erase the violent past.

The collection deals with contemporary politics, but also how we think about these questions, and the tools we use for social analysis. Some poems consider the relationship between (Global North-produced) social theory and local society. 'Foucault, Michel' reflects on the influence of the French thinker's ideas in Argentina, in particular his analyses of "los dispositivos / e instituciones de normalización" ["the apparatus / and the institutions of normalisation"], especially relevant to an Argentina living under or recovering from military rule, in which education was used as a form of coercive discipline and control. One thinks of Foucault's work on the development of systems of imprisonment and surveillance, as set down in *Surveiller et punir: Naissance de la prison* (1975, *Discipline and Punish: The Birth of the Prison*, 1977). Yet the poem pauses on a contradiction: Foucault's ideas were developed within the context of a strong public education system, at the heart of a (once) imperial power; in an ironic contrast in Argentina, they were received in the 1980s and 1990s "while the State was hollowed out" as education became subject to the currents of neoliberal capitalism, itself often perceived as an arm of neoimperialism.

The poem continues by challenging Foucault's critique of the discipline of elementary/primary schooling, with its neat rows,

---

9   On the history of Krupp, see for example James (2012).

individual desks, and corrective practices (in this case, obliging a left-handed child to write right-handed) by asking if the existence of an "escuela barrial", an implicitly modest neighbourhood school, in which the child receives a basic education, is really so worthy of disdain? Here, one might argue, we see in poetic form one of the conflicts that Raimondi attempted to balance in his role working for local government, between a theoretical critique of certain social formations and political practices, and their potential benefits for the local community.

As in *Poesía civil*, Raimondi delves into unlikely but revealing cultural coincidences. The poem 'Clinker', named after a material in the cement-making process, begins by describing J. M. W. Turner's 'Juliet and her Nurse' (1836). The painting was widely criticized in its day for moving the setting of Shakespeare's play to Venice from Verona and the apparent jumble of images in the background (Smiles 2007, 13). Its critics refused to accept that, as Raimondi's poem puts it, "la verdad ofrecida por el gran arte / está más allá de las contingencias del tiempo y espacio" ["the truth of great art / reaches beyond all the contingencies of time and space"].

This subject takes up the first 11 lines, over two long sentences. The next eight lines – one sentence – describe the industrial process of making cement, and in particular the cooling of clinker on grills. What is described, of course, appears also removed in time and space from Turner's painting, just as the cement produced will be removed in time and space (transported) for (future) profit. Another eight lines describe, simultaneously, the growing value of a cement magnate's fortune, and the purchase, by his heir, of Turner's painting. The heir in question was Amalia Lacroze de Fortabat, popularly known in Argentina as 'La dama del cemento' (Lady Cement), who purchased the canvas in 1980, for around $7 million (Santis 2012).

The key to the production of cement, states the poem, is the care with which explosions are used to loosen the mineral from its deposits during the mining process. These explosions are contrasted, in the last four lines of the poem, to the "cohetes anacrónicos" ["anachronistic rockets"] in Turner's painting, "signo avieso / en definitivo, de superar el silencio forzoso de la pintura" ["a perverse sign of overcoming painting's forced silence"].

Turner's fireworks, an apparent anachronism that still exercises specialists, are a noisy and spectacular excess in the painting, in contrast to the precise use of explosives in this particular extractive industry. The poem's irony is that time and space do not matter for the great truths revealed to us by art, but in this case the 'truth' is not that of art's transcendence or any similarly Romantic notion. Rather, art reveals the role of those holding the purse strings. The painting speaks to us, its explosions overcoming "el silencio forzoso" of paint on canvas, but what it says in Raimondi's poem is rather different from what contemporary critics might have claimed it was saying.

In 'Weil Brothers', Raimondi looks at another quirk of history typical of his poems. The title comes from the name of a major German-Argentine export company of the turn of the twentieth century. The first 22 lines of the poem focus on the success of the company, and in particular its ability to match local environmental conditions such as soil, and the availability of cheap labour, mainly recent Italian and Spanish immigrants, to demand on the world market. The last four lines point out that these profits went to finance, among other things, the "Escuela de Frankfurt", or Frankfurt School, and its attempts to overcome the orthodox Marxist vision of "base-superstructure".

This is, in simplified form, true: Félix José Weil (1898–1975), an Argentine-German Marxist, used large sums from the business fortune of his father, Hermann Weil, to fund the Institute for Social Research in Frankfurt, which he and Friedrich Pollock founded in 1923 (Jay 1973, 8, 10–11).[10] Like the Turner owned by an Argentine cement heiress, this historical curiosity – the role of Argentine industry in the development of European Marxist theory – reminds us of the inescapable presence of economic reality even in attempts to uncouple

---

10   It was a further quirk of history, noted by Jay (1973, 24), that Félix Weil's inheritance of the family firm on his father's death, and with it the obligation to return to Argentina to oversee affairs there, was a major obstacle to his taking over the directorship of the Institute.

from it. *Lexikón* goes even further than *Poesía civil* in its critical and critically self-aware analysis of contemporary culture.

On Translating Raimondi

[Ben:] As Ezra Pound put it, "great literature is simply language charged with meaning to the utmost possible degree" (1954: 23). The task of the translator is to ask, what are the forms of making meaning of a given text? This involves assessing priorities – which of rhythm, rhyme, form, shape, image, voice, layout, dominate the poem? What role does silence play?

An important consideration in translating Sergio's work, in particular into English, is the need to avoid the prosaic. Sergio very seldom runs clauses over a line-end even if he often has very long sentences. His poems are not simply 'cut-up prose' with arbitrary divisions; when he does employ enjambment in a clause, there is generally a good reason. He very rarely ends a line of verse on a preposition, conjunction, or other 'lesser' part of speech. These features often necessitate rearrangement of material, and our translation is therefore not always strictly line for line.

Sergio also employs a range of registers – for example mixing a voice and lexis that are distinctly colloquial with a more complex, even convoluted syntax. This has its roots in his classical studies, and his love of Latin poetry – in particular Catullus and Propertius – alongside his engagement with and understanding of culture in the broadest sense, with poetry as the site at which these interests can meet. High- and low-register terms, everyday and technical language, mingle through his poems. The voice is often subtle, at times ironic – as discussed above – and the translator must decide what to make explicit that is implicit, and what to leave subtly hinted at or alluded to, or left tellingly unsaid.

Research played an important part in the translation process. I travelled to Bahía Blanca on two occasions, interviewing Sergio and visiting both the Museo del Puerto and his house in the city. This 'visual background' was hugely useful for gaining a sense of the world the work – especially in *Poesía civil* – inhabits. Sergio answered questions about his poems, often in considerable depth, and also shared the research that informed them, including books and archival material. He also commented on drafts of phrases, lines and poems.

For each poem here included I produced an initial plain translation, including comments on technical difficulties and factual details in the poem. I had translated some of Sergio's work for the Poetry International Festival, Rotterdam (2016), and had these drafts. Mark then worked on his version to produce the measured verse translation. Both translators tweaked this, over successive rounds of corrections, to produce the version that readers can see.

* * *

[Mark:] Working on Sergio's poems during the lockdowns of 2020–2021, when many of the first drafts of these translations took shape, was a strange double experience. On one hand, sitting scribbling in a notebook by the bedroom window was as solitary an activity as could be. On the other, through the poems I felt connected in complex ways with my co-translator and to Sergio himself. I felt a strong sense of the force of his character and intellect.

Beyond that, the poems' subject matter made visible the strong but invisible links between Argentine grain, a Panamanian hotel, a Russian ship, a Chinese tech company, and the world seen from my window – smaller than ever, it seemed, but increasingly intricate.

My method, too, was a mix of the hermetic and the networked. Ben had sent me the originals and his literal versions in English. I took these a batch at a time and made a rough initial draft of my own using only the original text and a couple of dictionaries. When this was complete, I would turn to Ben's clear and helpfully annotated literals.

I made my first 'sketch' in each case independently to make sure I was responding directly to Sergio's text. After this exclusive dialogue with the work itself, I brought in the outside world through Ben's work and other sources. The greater insight and context they brought informed the path the translation took from that point.

It was interesting to see how often in difficult passages Ben and

I had independently chosen the same word or phrase. It reinforced my sense that the translation was arising out of a real conversation between the languages. I wondered to what extent this resulted from Sergio's own familiarity with English poetry.

Every translation forces practical decisions on the translator, from individual word choice up to the shape of the work on the page. My approach has always started from the premise that I would want to read a translation that comes as close as possible to transparency, so the reader can see the original as if through a pane of glass. But all glass bends the light, and in this case the refraction comes from my equally strong desire for a translation that speaks to me as a poem in English, that could stand alone even if there were no original version. This makes translation one of the most complex of activities – bound close to the source text, yet requiring much creativity.

To me, the 'feel' of poem is the link between the two imperatives of faithfulness to the text and poetic craft. The short poem 'Caballos en la vía pública' ['Horses in the Public Highway'] (*Poesía civil*) gives a demonstration of the need to listen with especial care to the textures of Sergio's voice. It begins with an exemplar of his understated irony and dry humour, and his ability to focus on a single detail that implies a complex and deeply understood context:

> Una reglamentación referida a los horarios
> en los que es lícito que un decimonónico caballo
> haga resonar sus herrajes en la vía pública, eso
> es el poder.

> A regulation governing the hours
> during which a nineteenth-century horse
> may click its hooves on public highways, that
> is power.

It then presents a syntactical challenge – the rubbish gatherers riding on their cart are suddenly elevated by the diction: in phrasing the action "sentados van" the line inverts the usual word order in Spanish, giving this moment an unexpected regality. I had to find a way of recreating this effect in English that did not throw the reader off completely. Eventually I chose the verb 'proceed' as quite distinct from simply 'go' or 'ride':

> aquellos capaces de distinguir la rentabilidad
> en lo que el resto de los vecinos considera inútil
> sentados van sobre un tablón con las riendas
> en la mano

> those capable of seeing the value
> in what the neighbours consider useless
> proceed, seated on a board with the reins
> in their hands

Further into the poem, the tone changes dramatically, clashing the restraint and implied self-possession of the workers with the callous, short-term vision of the modern cleaning truck, "which, democratically, doesn't give a damn."

It is this capacity for each poem to take in so many dimensions of subject, tone and language that renders Sergio's work so fascinating and so rewarding to translate.

I did not attempt to recreate the versification of the original poems, unwilling to force English into Spanish and Latin classical meters. However, to resort to free verse so as to strictly follow the sense and the lineation of the originals would sacrifice an essential part of the original text, as the shape of the lines carries its own weight in the poems' meaning and sound. Instead, I generally aimed for broadly iambic lines. These were most commonly pentameter, English alexandrine, or the Elizabethan 'fourteener'.

Imposing this structure on the poems did mean having to think carefully about syntax and word choice, and to be prepared to adjust the lineation at every step. The clearest example of this is in 'Blake, William' (*Lexikón*), where in order to create an English poem in English meter that still contained the ideas of the original text, I had to rearrange the lines considerably, radically rebuilding the original draft several times. The poems and the translations are therefore not mirrors of each other. However, though each took time and work to bring to their present state, I always felt that each arose organically from the original text. Even where Ben made adjustments and corrections, the solutions never seemed too far to seek. Since beginning this project I've felt a strong sympathy with Sergio's work, and I hope that this is visible in these versions.

* * *

Some more concrete examples will make clearer the issues at play. In certain cases, the problems we encountered are very specific to English. For example, one of the first poems translated, 'Ante un ejemplar de *Defense of Poetry*' ['Before a copy of *Defense of Poetry*'] (*Poesía civil*) it seems that Sergio tries to echo the English syntax; it is difficult to recreate the strangeness of this when the text returns to English. Notice for example phrases like "el otro quedó para tus lectores" ["the other was left to your readers"] or the multiple adjectives in a sentence like "el reino preferido, el invariable, intangible / y perfectamente ideal" ["the preferred kingdom, perfectly ideal / unchanging and intangible"]. Sergio writes in a calque of English, translating phrases from Percy Bysshe Shelley's *Defense*, which we of course consulted extensively. We respected as much as possible the syntax of the original, with the intention of maintaining the sensation of reading a text that had been translated, perhaps multiple times. Hence the somewhat grandiloquent beginning in English – "Written it is in your pages".

One particular difficulty – and one that we discussed at length with Sergio – was that of technical terms. We worked with search engines, Google Images and technical dictionaries, and consulted with colleagues and contacts – biologists, engineers and so on – to understand certain aspects of the lexicon Raimondi uses. This is a product of the research that Raimondi himself puts into each poem, often building up folders' worth of material for each composition, requiring a parallel effort on the part of the translator.

Some terms that Raimondi uses are very specific, presenting particular challenges. An example can be found in 'Zafra' (Harvest, *Lexikón*), and a problem with the measure used, the "arroba". This is a traditional measure in the Spanish-speaking world (around 11.5kg, or 25lb), and it is important not to get the weight wrong, otherwise the result might be absurd. But there is also an equivalence between the amount of sugar and the number of words in the speech, and with it a repetition of the figure 45. An earlier version opted for "ton" – 45 tons. But that is too small a quantity. Another option was to change it to five hundred, and with that to change the number of words to fifty thousand words – so an even longer speech. After some discussion, we decided that fidelity to the original measure was the best choice, despite its unfamiliarity to an anglophone audience: "forty-five thousand *arrobas*".

Perhaps the thorniest technical question came in the poem 'Modificación en la alimentación de las locomotoras fabricadas en Europa' ['Modification to the Fuel of Locomotives Built in Europe'] (*Poesía civil*), and in particular a phrase that describes, simultaneously, the function of a locomotive motor, and the energy of a poem:

> ...fuerza y presión
> del vapor acumulado en la caldera, arrojado
> sobre los émbolos en los cilindros que lleva
> sobre el liso riel dinámica a la rueda, que gira

> the force and pressure
> of steam accumulating in the boiler thrown
> onto the pistons in the cylinders and moved
> down the smooth dynamic rod to the wheel, which turns.

When consulted, Sergio pointed us in the direction of a fragment from a technical manual, by José Pipino, *El maquinista ferroviario* (*The Railway Engineer* Vol. II) (Talleres Gráficos R. Canals, 1930). He had read the book when researching for the poem, in the Railway Workers Union Library in Ingeniero White, as well as talking to retired workers he met there. Raimondi's explanation, and the source, were vital to getting both the technical terms and the sense of movement in the lines. Raimondi commented in an email on the irony of British translators consulting Argentine manuals and an Argentine poet to see how a 1930s British locomotive worked.

There is also the difficulty of cultural references. An example from the poem 'Sileno en la estación de ferrocarril' ['Silenus at the Railway Station'] (*Poesía civil*) is the term 'Tetra-brik'. This is a trademark around the world, but for English speakers, and especially the British, it is associated more with the consumption of milk and fruit juice rather than with alcohol, and in this case wine, which is what "Sileno" drinks. In a preliminary version, the word became 'cartons', but Sergio questioned whether 'cartons' would be understood to mean wine. The final version uses "litres", which is more elegant than, for example, adding a gloss ('of wine' – since it is implicit in the description) or changing it to bottles.

A further very important aspect here is the use of colloquial, oral interventions. For example, in 'Fish Block' (*Lexikón*), in the second verse, we read the phrase "a ver, más específicamente": a change of tone, and even of register, that must be captured in a word or two. It also changes the rhythm. After conversations with Sergio, we tried several options before arriving at the final version, "well, more specifically". Another fascinating feature of this poem is its rhythmic mimicry of the movement of fish in the sea.

'Autor (Als Produzent, Der)' (*Lexikón*) mixes political discourse, even dogma, and oral forms. The final sentence proved difficult, too, in particular to find phrasing that could be pronounced in English conversation, while keeping certain unexpected aspects of the original – the "clac clac" of his camera, without commas, which we kept in English as "click click".

In the poem 'Valençay' *(Lexikón)*, the final phrase – an ironic kick to the piece as a whole – reads, "Se aconseja acompañarlo con un Shiraz", a generic phrase from marketing in the food and drink industry – one that could be read on a supermarket shelf or a packaging label. This allows the translator a certain liberty, leading to our addition of "nice" to describe – in suitably bland terms – the bottle that goes with the cheese.

Another example is one of the sweetest poems in the collection, revealing a different aspect of Sergio's poetics, 'El poeta menor ante el nacimiento de su hijo' ['The Minor Poet on the Birth of His Son']

(*Poesía civil*). Like every poem in this selection, it is formally rigorous, with a sculpted shape, but it is also very funny on the struggles of a new family to bring some order to their professional and domestic routines. There is a long list of "temas" or "matters" that the couple has to talk about, which are quite formal ways of summarizing a typical domestic disagreement, and then a phrase, perfect in the Spanish, which is "amables formas de imponer distancia a los abuelos". Oral phrases give the translator a certain freedom, but also an obligation, because the translation must sound like something a person would say in real life; in this case there is the addition of a certain faux formality, maintained in the phrasing throughout the poem, and part of its subtle, self-deprecating humour.

Domestic speech in Spanish, because of the influence of Latin and for other reasons, can sound too formal to the British ear. A Colombian friend of Ben's can sometimes be heard saying to his teenage daughter, "no me desautorices" (lit. "don't de-authorize me" or "don't take away my authority"), which in English would be something like "don't you talk back to me" or even "don't give me any cheek". In this poem, in keeping with the wry overall tone, we rendered Raimondi's phrase as "friendly ways of keeping the grandparents at bay".

* * *

From international trade to critical theory, from national gastronomic traditions to the tribulations of family life: these last four examples capture the range and scale of Sergio Raimondi's poetry. We are all part of networks of politics, economics, and culture that extend way beyond what we can see, in time and space. This order of things is today characterised by growing inequality, injustice, and environmental degradation. The brilliance of these two collections is to give us a sense of how and where we fit, and to challenge us to ask what we might do to make things better.

BIBLIOGRAPHY

Works by Sergio Raimondi

2022. *Lexikón*. Buenos Aires: Mansalva.

2017. *Poesía civil / Zivilpoesie*. Translated by Timo Berger. Berlin: Reinecke and Voß.

2014. "Hacer política cultural es hacer política." Facebook post, 2015. https://www.facebook.com/sr.raimondi/posts/725284647541152

2013. Del Mercado mundial actual y las leyes sempiternas de la teoría de los géneros en Lukács. In *Estéticas de la dispersión*, edited by Franco Ingrassia, 13–22. Rosario: Beatriz Viterbo.

2012. *Für ein kommentiertes Wörterbuch*. Translated by Timo Berger. Berlin: Berenberg.

2011. Égloga del electrocardiograma. *Luz artificial* 1.1: 14–20.

2010. Poesía y división internacional del trabajo. Sobre *Estudios económicos* de J. B. Alberdi. *Revista planta* 1. http://plantarevista.com.ar/anteriores/nr1/raimondi.html

2007. El sistema afecta la lengua. Sobre la poesía de Martín Gambarotta. *Márgenes/Margens* 9: 50–59.

2005. *Zivilpoesie / Poesía Civil*. Translated by Timo Berger. Berlin: WVB.

2001. Alexis y Corydón a eso de las 3.15am. In *Monstruos. Antología de la joven poesía argentina*, edited by Arturo Carrera, 149–53. Buenos Aires: FCE.

2001. *Poesía civil*. Bahía Blanca: VOX/Senda.

1999. *Catulito*. Bahía Blanca: VOX.

1993. Viernes. *Diario de Poesía* 27: 9.

1990. Untitled selection of poems. *Diario de Poesía* 14: 26.

Raimondi, Sergio, Tulio Halperín Donghi, Horacio González, Alan Pauls, María Teresa Gramuglio, Nicolás Rosa, Julio Schvartzman, Laura Milano, Sylvia Saítta, Nora Avaro and Analía Capdevila. 2005. *Los clásicos argentinos, Sarmiento-Hernández-Borges-Arlt: los cuatro máximos escritores nacionales según once ensayistas contemporáneos*. Rosario: EMR.

Other Works

Adorno, Theodor. 2004. *Aesthetic Theory*. Translated by Robert Hullot-Kentor. London: Continuum.

Bollig, Ben. 2016. *Politics and Public Space in Contemporary Argentine Poetry. The Lyric and the State*. New York: Palgrave Macmillan.

Ceresa, Constanza. 2015. 'Tomas para un Documental' ['Shots for a Documentary')] and the Thick Framing of History. *Liminalities* 11.3. Accessed Jan 13, 2016. http://liminalities.net/11-3/tomas.pdf

Ceresa, Constanza. 2011. Conversations with Martín Gambarotta (May–September 2010). Translated by Katy Critchfield. *Journal of Latin American Cultural Studies* 20.3: 197–216.

Di Leone, Luciana. 2014. *Poesia e escolhas afetivas*. Rio de Janeiro: Rocco.

Fondebrider, Jorge (ed.). 2008. *Una antología de la poesía argentina (1970–2008)*. Santiago de Chile: LOM.

Fondebrider, Jorge (ed.). 2006. *Tres décadas de poesía argentina 1976–2006*. Buenos Aires: Libros del Rojas.

French, Jennifer L. 2005. *Nature, Neo-Colonialism, and the Spanish American Regional Writers*. Hanover, NH: Dartmouth College Press.

James, Harold. 2012. *Krupp: A History of the Legendary German Firm*. Princeton: Princeton University Press.

Jay, Martin. 1973. *The Dialectical Imagination: A History of the Frankfurt School and the Institute for Social Research*. London: Heinemann.

Kesselman, Violeta, Ana Mazzoni and Damián Selci (eds). 2012. *La tendencia materialista. Antología crítica de la poesía de los 90*. Buenos Aires: Paradiso.

Mazzoni, Ana, and Damián Selci. 2006. Poesía actual y cualquierización. In *Tres décadas de poesía argentina 1976–2006*, edited by Jorge Fondebrider, 257–68. Buenos Aires: Libros del Rojas.

Pas, Hernán. 2007. Una materialidad de la exasperación. Acerca de *Poesía civil*, de Sergio Raimondi. *Orbis Tertius* XII.13: 1–8.

Perlongher, Néstor. 1992. Argentina's Secret Poetry Boom. Translated by Margaret Smallman. *Travesia. Journal of Latin American Cultural Studies* 1.2: 178–84.

Porrúa, Ana. 2011. *Caligrafía tonal: ensayos sobre poesía*. Buenos Aires: Entropía.

Pound, Ezra. 1954. How to Read. In *Literary Essays of Ezra Pound* edited with an introduction by T. S. Eliot, London: Faber and Faber, pp. 15–40.

Prieto, Martín. 1996. La zanjita. Review of *Poesía en la fisura*, edited by Daniel Freidemberg. *Diario de Poesía* 36: 29.

Revista Mancilla. 2012. Tensiones para pensar la política cultural. Entrevista a Sergio Raimondi. Gestión pública y cultura. *Revista Mancilla* 2.5: 73–77. http://www.centrocultural.coop/blogs/contentio/2013/10/entrevista-a-sergio-raimondi-gestion-publica-y-cultura/

Santis, Juan Pablo de. 2012. Amalita, la dama del cemento. *La Nación*, Feb 20, 2012. http://www.lanacion.com.ar/1449858-amalita-la-dama-del-cemento

Smiles, Sam. 2007. *J. M. W. Turner: The Making of a Modern Artist*. Manchester: Manchester University Press.

Svampa, Maristella. 2014. Revisiting Argentina 2001–2013. From '¡Que se vayan todos! to the Peronist Decade. In *Argentina since the 2001 Crisis: Recovering the Past, Reclaiming the Future*, edited by Cara Levey, Daniel Ozarow and Chris Wylde, 155–73. Basingstoke: Palgrave Macmillan.

Yuszczuk, Marina. 2007–2008. Almas discretas, objetos particulares. Sobre el conocimiento de y a partir de los objetos en la poesía de Lucía Blanco y Sergio Raimondi. *BOLETÍN del Centro de Estudios de Teoría y Crítica Literaria* 13/14: 1–10.

Zaidenwerg, Ezequiel. (ed.). 2014. *Penúltimos. 33 Poetas de Argentina*. Mexico City: UNAM.

A Note on Sources and Previous Publications

Poesía civil was published by VOX/Senda, Bahía Blanca, in 2000. *Lexikón* was published by Mansalva of Buenos Aires in 2022; some of the poems, in earlier form, appeared in *Für ein kommentiertes Wörterbuch / Para un diccionario crítico de la lengua,* translated by Timo Berger (Berlin: Berenberg, 2012).

Ben has written on Raimondi in his book *Politics and Public Space in Contemporary Argentine Poetry: The Lyric and the State* (New York: Palgrave Macmillan, 2016). A small selection of these poems were published – in earlier translations, by Ben, in *Contemporary Argentine Poetry. A Bilingual Selection* (Buenos Aires: Eloísa Cartonera, 2010). Ben translated a selection of poems and wrote a brief biography of Raimondi for the Poetry International Festival, Rotterdam, 2016. Five of the poems, in translation by us both, were published in *Latin American Literature Today* in March 2022.

SERGIO RAIMONDI: SELECTED POEMS

POESÍA CIVIL

CIVIL POETRY

DE LA LENGUA Y EL ARTE COMO CAPITAL

ANTE UN EJEMPLAR DE *DEFENSE OF POETRY* CON EL SELLO "PACIFIC RAILWAY LIBRARY, B. BCA., NO 815 (TO BE RETURNED WITHIN 14 DAYS)"

Escrito está en tus páginas
que poesía y principio de propiedad
dos fuerzas son que se repelen,
pero escrito está también
que la poesía es infinita y divina,
no hay tiempo preciso ni lugar,
y el dominio que te concierne
verdadero es, eterno, único,
imperio sobre el universo todo.
Oh, legislador del mundo,
no fuiste ignorado en absoluto,
es sólo que fuiste considerado
tal como exigías: se te dio el reino
preferido, el invariable, intangible
y perfectamente ideal;
el otro quedó para tus lectores,
dueños y destinados a regir
territorios más concretos del planeta.

ON ART AND LANGUAGE AS CAPITAL

BEFORE A COPY OF *DEFENSE OF POETRY* WITH A STAMP, "PACIFIC RAILWAY LIBRARY, BAHIA BLANCA, NO. 815 (TO BE RETURNED WITHIN 14 DAYS)"

Written it is in your pages
that poetry and property
are two repelling principles
but it is also written there
that poetry is infinite, divine,
it has no precise time or place
and the kingdom that concerns you
is true, eternal and unique,
empire of all the universe.
Oh legislator of the world,
you weren't unacknowledged at all
only that you were considered
just as you required: you received
the preferred kingdom, perfectly ideal
unchanging and intangible;
the other left to your readers,
masters and destined to govern
more concrete parts of the planet.

GLOSA *A ODE TO A NIGHTINGALE* DE JOHN KEATS

El dolor en el corazón está. La modorra
también, ahí en el jardín, bajo el ciruelo,
sentado en la silla que tomó de la mesa
del desayuno. Pero no ha habido té.
Tragos fuertes a las tres de la mañana,
unas cuantas copas encima, boca mojada
y fuga entre la espesura de mayo, fuga,
como si eso fuera deseable, hacia la nada:
amnesia, quejas entre los reflejos prestados
del cielo, esas cosas. Se levanta y se mueve
hacia la fronda: lo más delicado no se ve,
se oye apenas o, mejor, sólo por el aroma
se distingue: y entre espinos y frutales,
entre el aromo, la violeta y la eglantina
persigue entre las sombras la sombra
de quien canta por los siglos para todos.
Bueno, no para todos. El jardinero duerme.
Hubo temprano la tormenta que vendrá
y el hombre, dicen, tuvo bastante trabajo:
podó árboles y cercas, amontonó ramas
en la hoguera, frutos podridos, una o dos
alondras en el estanque caídas y fue
el único en toda la casa que se acostó
con el pelo compacto de briznas y humo.
Dejó la Naturaleza parecida a un poema

GLOSS ON *ODE TO A NIGHTINGALE*
BY JOHN KEATS

The ache in the heart is there. The numbness
too, in the garden under the plum tree,
sat on the chair he took from the breakfast
table. But it's not tea he's been having.
Strong drink at three o'clock in the morning,
a few of them downed already, moist mouth
and escape through the May thicket, escape
towards nothing, as if that were desirable:
forgetfulness, groans among the loaned lights
of the sky, those things. He rises and moves
towards green: the most subtle things unseen,
barely heard, or, let's say, only distinguished
by their scent: amid hawthorns and fruit trees,
the musk-rose, violet and eglantine,
he pursues through the shadows the shadow
who's sung across the ages for us all.
Well, not 'us all'. The gardener's asleep.
The storm that was forecast arrived early
and this man, it's said, had a lot of work:
he pruned trees and hedges, heaped up branches
in the fire, some rotten fruit, one or two
drowned larks fallen in the tank, and he was
the only one in the house who lay down
with his hair compact with clippings and smoke.
He left Nature looking like a poem,

y se cansó, claro. Ahora nada siente, nada,
nada oye ni oirá hasta el sol: melodía ninguna.
Es que está muerto y literal y, encima, ronca:
zzzzzzzzzzzzzzzzzzzzzzzzzzzzzzzzzzzzzz
zzzzzzzzzzzzzzzzzzzzzzzzzzzzzzzzzz
zzzzzzzzzzzzzzzzzzzzzzzzzzzzzzzzzzzzzzzz.
Amanece. No hay música en el mundo.
El jardinero se levanta, se dispone a buscar
sus herramientas y ve, al acercarse a la casa,
derrumbado al jovencito en la silla al sol.
¿Estará despierto o dormido el poeta?
Que descanse, shhh, que descanse ahora.

was worn out, of course. Now he feels nothing,
hears nothing, nor will, until dawn: no melody.
He's dead to the world, literal, snoring:
ZZZZZZZZZZZZZZZZZZZZZZZZZZZZZZZZZZZZ
ZZZZZZZZZZZZZZZZZZZZZZZZZZZZZZZZZ
ZZZZZZZZZZZZZZZZZZZZZZZZZZZZZZZZZZZZZZ.
It's dawn. Fled is the music of the world.
The gardener gets up, sets to looking
for his tools and sees, approaching the house,
the young man in his chair, slumped in the sun.
Will the poet be awake, or sleeping?
Let him rest now, shhhhhh, let him rest for now.

SILENO EN LA ESTACIÓN DE FERROCARRIL

Acostado de lado, con un codo incómodo
apoyado en el cemento y la cabeza
tirada hacia atrás, duerme. Rodillas dobladas,
pies contra el culo, al aire la panza enorme,
boca abierta al cielo, chata nariz.
Esto es obra de dos o tres tetra-brik.
Si fuera de mármol estaría expuesto
en un museo de Roma, Londres o París
como ejemplo de arte helenístico.
Y no le molestarían las moscas.

SILENUS AT THE RAILWAY STATION

Laid on one side, on an awkward elbow
supported by the cement, and his head
lolling back, he sleeps. His knees bent double,
feet against his arse, airing that belly,
mouth open to the sky, a nose squashed flat.
This is the work of two or three litres.
If in marble, he'd be exhibited
in a museum – Rome, London, Paris –
an example of Hellenistic art.
And he would have no trouble with the flies.

LA VIANDA BAJO LA LUPA

W

El New York Times, en su sección económica,
destacó su llegada como una gran renovación
para la industria petroquímica. Fue construida
por la compañía Ishikawajima en un astillero
próximo a Nagoya, Japón, utilizando tecnología
de la corporación norteamericana Union Carbide.
Montada en una plataforma de veinte metros
por ochenta y nueve, y tras haber atravesado
el océano en dos meses sobre un buque holandés
sin que las puntas de sus pies acaricien las olas,
reina en el sector de muelles de Puerto Galván
y en la mente de los más cotizados ingenieros:
en comparación a una planta en tierra utiliza
un cuarto de energía, un décimo de las áreas
necesarias para su instalación y, en particular,
implica la mitad del costo general de inversión.
Su capacidad de producción es de ciento veinte
mil toneladas anuales. Su núcleo es un reactor
UNIPOL que explota en la noche para anunciar
que no habrá ya vuelta atrás hacia la inercia.
Su nombre es síntesis de la palabra waterborne.

FOOD UNDER THE MAGNIFYING GLASS

W

The New York Times took note in its business section
of the plant's arrival as a great leap forward
for the petrochemical sector. It was built
by the Ishikawajima Company based
near Nagoya, Japan, using technology
from the North American Union Carbide Corp.
Mounted on a platform 20 metres across
by 89 long, and after having travelled
the sea in two months on a Dutch vessel
without its toes so much as caressing the waves
it rules among the wharves of Puerto Galván
and in the minds of the most valued engineers:
compared with a plant on land it uses
one-fourth of the power, a tenth of the area
for its installation, and in particular
saves fifty percent in the total investment.
Production capacity is 120
thousand tonnes a year. Its core is a UNIPOL
reactor that explodes in the night to announce
that there's no going back towards inertia.
Its name is short for the word *waterborne*.

QUÉ ES EL MAR

El barrido de una red de arrastre a lo largo del lecho,
mallas de apertura máxima, en el tanque setecientos mil
litros de gas-oil, en la bodega bolsas de papa y cebolla,
jornada de treinta y cinco horas, sueño de cuatro, café,
acuerdos pactados en oficinas de Bruselas, crecimiento
del calamar illex en relación a la temperatura del agua
y las firmas de aprobación de la Corte Suprema, circuito
de canales de acero inoxidable por donde el pescado cae,
abadejo, hubbsi, transferencias de permiso amparadas
por la Secretaría de Agricultura, Ganadería y Pesca; ahí:
atraviesa el fresquero la línea imaginaria del paralelo, va
tras una mancha en la pantalla del equipo de detección,
ignorante el cardumen de la noción de millas o charteo,
de las estadísticas irreales del INIDEP o el desfasaje
entre jornal y costo de vida desde el año mil novecientos
noventa y dos, filet de merluza de cola, SOMU y pez rata,
cartas de crédito adulteradas, lámparas y asiático pabellón,
irrupción de brotes de aftosa en rodeos británicos, hoki,
retorno a lo más hondo de toneladas de pota muerta
ante la aparición de langostino (valor cinco veces mayor),
infraestructura de almacenamiento y frío, caladero, eso.

WHAT IS THE SEA

The sweep of a trawler net across the length of the bed,
mesh at maximum, in the tank seven hundred thousand
litres of fuel, below bags of potatoes and onions,
shifts lasting thirty-five hours, then sleep for four, some coffee,
agreements signed in offices in Brussels, increasing
illex squid in proportion to the water temperature
and the approvals signed in the Supreme Court, a circuit
of channels made of stainless steel into which the catch falls,
pollock, hake, permit transfers being made with approval
from the Agriculture and Fisheries Ministry; there:
the fishing boat crosses the imaginary line, goes
after a stain on the screen of the detector machine,
the shoal ignorant of the notion of miles or charter,
of the made-up Fisheries Institute stats or the gap
between wages and living costs since 1992,
the long-tailed hake fillet, Seamen's Union and rattail,
faked credit letters, lamps and Asian flag of convenience,
the outbreak of foot and mouth among British herds, hoki,
chucking back to the very depths tons of dead cuttlefish
when langoustine (which has five times greater value) appears,
storage infrastructure and cold, and fishing ground, all that.

CRACKER 2 O MONIMENTA MINISTRI

Lo que hay allá, entre las figuras de humo
que se disuelven contra el fondo más oscuro
y la oscilación de las llamas en el horizonte,
es la ley catorce siete ochenta de Inversiones
y Radicaciones de Capitales Extranjeros
promulgada por el gobierno de A. Frondizi
a fines de los sesenta y evidencia innegable
de que nada surge cualquier día de la nada.
Y aunque los ojos vean sólo el espectáculo
de millares de luces cayendo sobre el metal
o, si se tiene la estrecha conciencia del día,
el carácter perjudicial de vapores que suben,
lo que se habrá de percibir en el Cracker 2
es el monumento levantado a la victoria
de las medidas tomadas por Martínez de Hoz
durante sus primeros tres años de gobierno:
reducción de los aranceles de importación,
ley de transferencia de tecnología, liberación
generalizada de los mercados, subvaluación
del dólar, aumento de la jornada de trabajo,
racionalización de los procesos productivos,
elevada manipulación de las tasas de interés.
Ya llega por el gasoducto el etano. Ya ingresa
al horno tras atravesar bajo tierra la ciudad:
temperatura máxima para el fraccionamiento
de las moléculas y sus mutaciones en el valor.

CRACKER 2 OR MONIMENTA MINISTRI

What is there, between the figures of smoke
that dissolve against the darker background
and the flames' movement on the horizon
is Law 14/7/80: Investments
and Establishment of Foreign Capital
by the government of A. Frondizi
in the late 60s, incontrovertible proof
that nothing comes overnight from nowhere.
And although the eyes see only the spectacle
of thousands of lights falling on metal,
or, with the broader awareness of day,
the damaging nature of rising fumes,
what one should detect there in Cracker 2
is a monument to the victory
of steps taken by Martínez de Hoz
during his first three years in government:
reduction of the tariffs on imports,
the law on technology transfer, full
market liberalisation, dollar
devaluation, lengthening of the workday,
rationalisation of production,
high-level interest rate manipulation.
Ethanol rises through the duct, arrives
in the furnace having passed below ground:
maximum temperature for fractioning
molecules, and their mutable value.

GRAMSCI Y VALÉRY EN LA BIBLIOTECA
DEL CÍRCULO DE ESTUDIOS SOCIALES CREADO
EN INGENIERO WHITE EN 1899 POR EL GRUPO
ANARQUISTA 'LIBRES PENSADORES'

Parte de lo que hay, en la estructura de los andamios
que sostiene a los pintores de los tanques de la ESSO,
es un problema de sintaxis: ni mucho más ni mucho menos.

GRAMSCI AND VALERY IN THE LIBRARY
OF THE CIRCLE OF SOCIAL STUDIES
ESTABLISHED IN INGENIERO WHITE IN 1899
BY THE ANARCHIST GROUP 'FREE THINKERS'

Part of what there is, in the structure of the scaffolding
that supports the painters working on the tanks of ESSO,
is a syntactical problem: not much more, not much less.

LITERATURA Y OTRAS CUESTIONES DE MENOR IMPORTANCIA

EL GRILLO INCOMPRENDIDO

Como si se le hubiera hecho difícil soportar
la fama de su cotidiana capacidad musical,
el grillo que habita la casa desde hace días
se niega a frotar la textura ondeada de un ala
contra el afilado borde de la otra en el ejercicio
que vaya a saber desde cuándo es conocido
como "canto", y se vuelve así algo temerario,
ya que por la semejanza de color, la inmovilidad
al encenderse la luz del baño, la falta de lentes
de quien se levanta en mitad de la noche
y la ausencia, como decía, de su sonido habitual,
se confunde con facilidad con una cucaracha.

LITERATURE AND OTHER QUESTIONS OF LESSER IMPORTANCE

THE MISUNDERSTOOD CRICKET

As if it had become difficult to endure
the fame of its everyday musical skill
the cricket that's been living in the house for days
refuses to rub the waved texture of one wing
against the sharp edge of the other to produce
the sound that has been referred to since who knows when
as its 'song', and become rather reckless, so that
due to its similar colour and its stillness
as the bathroom light goes on, the lack of glasses
of whoever's up in the middle of the night
and the absence, as I said, of its normal sound,
it is easily mistaken for a cockroach.

LA DIETA DE DANTE

La dietética debería preguntarse cómo un poeta
que basaba toda su alimentación en el huevo
(con una pizca de sal, según cuenta la fábula)
produjo tal cantidad de versos en forma regular
durante un tiempo considerable. La estructura
cerrada de la obra sin dudas fue un aliciente:
no se trataba de avanzar hacia la nada (o sí,
pero en todo caso la nada también había sido
prevista). Tal vez habría que tener en cuenta
la relación entre contenido energético y volumen
que favorece a este alimento si se lo compara,
por ejemplo, con la carne. En fin, los estudiosos
deberían entrar en cuestiones al parecer ajenas
y dedicarse por un tiempo al análisis de los versos
para corroborar, como un ruso señaló alguna vez,
el impulso con el que cada terceto presupone
y dispara al que le sigue según el modelo de fases
de un cohete espacial; es sólo una sugerencia,
pero la célula del huevo, es más que conocido,
contiene el germen de un nuevo ser y las sustancias
de las cuales se podría nutrir. Por otra parte,
un gran porcentaje de esos seres suelen ser aves.

DANTE'S DIET

Dieticians should ask how a poet
who based all his nourishment on the egg
(with a pinch of salt, so the story goes)
produced so much verse in regular form
for so long a time. The work's hermetic
structuring was doubtless an incentive:
it did not move toward nothing (or does,
but anyway the nothing also was
foreseen). Perhaps one ought to remember
calories' relationship to volume
that favours this food in comparison,
for example, to meat. Still, the experts
would have to explore strange-seeming questions
and spend some time analysing his lines
to confirm, as a Russian once observed,
the impulse with which each tercet predicts
and launches the next, like the phase model
of a rocket; it's just a suggestion
but the yolk of the egg, it's widely known,
contains the germ of a new life and substances
with which it can be nourished. However,
a large percentage of these lives are birds.

EL POETA MENOR ANTE EL NACIMIENTO
DE SU HIJO

Luego de hallar, tras días de búsqueda, el lápiz
en la cabina del camioncito de los bomberos,
y de comprobar la independencia de juicio
del heredero, que rompe las páginas predilectas
e intactas deja las indiferentes, el poeta menor
decide dialogar con su mujer sobre un tema clave:
la organización espacial y temporal de su labor,
en la casa, luego del nacimiento del hijo.
A lo largo de la conversación se tocan varios temas:
compra de comestibles y artículos de limpieza,
pago de impuestos, turnos para el cuidado,
diversión, alimentación e higiene del niño,
ausencia de cuidado, diversión, alimentación
e higiene de la pareja, necesidad de registrar
sus primeros pasos, frecuencia de uso del
– vulgarmente denominado – chupete,
amables formas de imponer distancia a los abuelos.
Cuando una mutua mudez evidencia el final,
el poeta menor comprueba que su inquietud
ha sido desplazada en vista de otras urgencias.
Esa noche, como un inspirado romántico
que aprovechase el silencio de los mortales
para dejar fluir el carácter alado de sus versos,
canta durante horas una canción de cuna.

THE MINOR POET ON THE BIRTH OF HIS SON

Having found – after days of searching – his pencil
hidden in the cabin of the toy fire engine,
and having witnessed the independent judgement
of his heir, who tears up the better pages
and spares the indifferent, the minor poet
decides to discuss a key matter with his wife:
organization of time and space for his work
in the house, after the birth of their son.
This conversation touches on many topics:
the purchase of groceries and cleaning products,
the payment of bills, taking turns minding the child,
ensuring fun, feeding and hygiene for the boy,
the absence of that fun, feeding, care and hygiene
for the two adults, the need to make a record
of the child's first steps, the frequency of use of
– to employ a vulgar term – the dummy,
friendly ways of keeping the grandparents at bay.
When a mutual silence indicates the ending,
the minor poet understands that his concerns
have been displaced by other considerations.
That night, like an inspiration-filled romantic
taking advantage of silence among mortals
to let flourish the winged spirit of his verses,
for hours and hours he sings a lullaby.

LA LITERATURA SERÁ SOMETIDA
A INVESTIGACIÓN (BRECHT, 1939)

Se trata de poner en tela de juicio la literatura
con criterios no creados por ella; o sea:
de tensar los versos ante la acción del fuego
y de calificarlos no con el lápiz sino con el cuchillo,
por ejemplo, o una sierra cariada o el carozo
de un durazno. Poesía y ferretería, destornillador
y vocal, metonimia a 220, en morsa la metáfora
a ser por el toc ajustada del martillo.
Las herramientas no están terminadas aún.
Y quien cree que se trabaja día a día en ellas,
chispas de la soldadora entre almanaques amarillos,
vidrio y alcohol entre fórmulas erradas,
salsa y serrucho en patios, galpones y cocinas
de casas ubicadas fuera del radio de la urbe
o en el centro mismo de su fragor cotidiano
un poco desvaría y se engaña.

LITERATURE WILL BE SUBJECTED TO INVESTIGATION (BRECHT, 1939)

It's about debating literature
with criteria not designed by it;
that's to say, tensing lines before a fire,
rating them not with pencil but a knife
for instance, a rusty saw, or the stone
of a peach. Poetry and ironwork,
screwdriver and vowel, metonym set
at 220v, a vice
round a metaphor being hammered straight.
The tools for the job are not finished yet.
and whoever thinks they're worked on daily,
solder sparks among yellow almanacs,
glass, alcohol among failed formulae,
sauce and saws in patios, hangars and kitchens
in houses far beyond the urban zone
or in the centre of its daily din
is a little crazy and deluded.

HOY COCINA MATSUO BASHŌ

El maestro dijo "pimienta más alas igual libélula"
no al revés, no se trataría de sacar alas a la libélula
para abandonar en el aire un aromático grano
que por su propio peso caería. No, ¡la gracia es dar
vuelo al fruto para que alto se eleve desde la mesa!
Pero a veces urge cualquier picante para otorgar
gusto a la salsa que sobre la hornalla hierve
y no hay más que esa libélula o figura de lenguaje
dando vueltas por ahí y hasta molestando un poco.
El maestro, ya con delantal, debería abandonar
la elegancia de la anécdota para tener en cuenta
tanto su propio apetito como el de los comensales;
el juicio poético podrá o no condenar la acción,
pero el estómago sabrá agradecerlo en la cena.
Y no es de extrañar que, de ser la cocción justa,
la digestión se cumpla entre platos, ollas y vapores
con el sentimiento preciado de gracia y levedad.

TODAY MATSUO BASHŌ COOKS

The Master said 'a pepper plus wings equal dragonfly'
not the reverse, it's not about plucking its wings
to abandon mid-air an aromatic grain
that on its own would fall. No, the trick is to give
flight to the fruit so it rises from the table!
But at times something spicy is needed to give
taste to the sauce that's boiling on the hob
and there's nothing but that dragonfly or conceit
flying around and even slightly annoying.
The master, now wearing his apron, should give up
the anecdote's elegance while keeping in mind
as much his appetite as that of those dining;
poetic judgment may condemn – or not – the act,
but the stomach will enjoy it in the dinner.
And it's no surprise that, if the cooking is right,
digestion will take place among plates, pans and steam
with a pleasant sense of grace and lightness.

LOS ARTESANOS

PARA HACER UNA TORTA SIN LECHE

La cocción tendrá que ver con el tipo de horno,
como todo: se recomienda un fuego mínimo, lento
de entre cuarenta y cuarenta y cinco minutos,
pero cada cocina, como cada molde, es particular
y es inútil establecer una medida exacta para todos.
Yo digo: una taza de té con leche de aceite de maíz
(no mezcla), una y media (casi dos) de azúcar, bol
y batir, batir: ladeado el recipiente y paleta el brazo
o la máquina en su punto máximo. Ah, dos huevos
además, y bien batido todo hasta espesar la mezcla.
Entonces se agregan dos tazas de agua hirviendo.
Se levantará una espuma. Se deja reposar un rato.
Mientras, se mezclan aparte tres tazas de harina
(pasada antes por el cernidor) con una cucharada
de Royal y otra de bicarbonato (puede ser menos,
más, se ve). Sumar todo y batir. Muy suavemente:
hay que lograr que la masa pierda consistencia.
El resto se sabe: enmantecar el molde, enharinarlo
y horno. Titi Trujillo le echa un chorrito de vino
oporto. Titina Lancioni a veces licor de café o esencia
de vainilla. Otros le ponen trozos de manzana,
pasas de uva, chocolate o ciruela. Eso va en gustos,
en las ganas de inventar, en lo que se tenga a mano.

THE ARTISANS

TO MAKE A CAKE WITHOUT MILK

The method will depend on the type of oven,
as with everything: low heat is recommended, slow
for approximately forty to forty-five minutes,
but each kitchen, like each tin, is particular
and it's useless to set an exact measure for all.
I suggest a milky-teacupful of maize oil
(don't mix), one and a half (near two) of sugar, bowl
and whisk, whisk: tilt the container stiffen the arm
or set the machine to maximum. Oh, two eggs
as well, and whisked well until the mixture thickens.
Then add two cupfuls of boiling water.
A foam will appear. Let it rest a while.
Meanwhile, mix separately three cupfuls of flour
(this should already be well sieved) with a spoonful
of Royal, one of bicarbonate (could be less,
more, take a look). Mix it and whisk. Very gently:
you have to make the batter lose consistency.
The rest you will know: grease the tin, dust it with flour,
and oven. Titi Trujillo adds a small glass
of port. Titina Lancioni, liqueur or vanilla
essence. Others put in apple slices,
raisins, chocolate, or plums. It depends on taste,
on your inventiveness, or what you've got to hand.

MEDITACIÓN SOBRE LAS ESTADÍSTICAS DE EMBARQUE[1]

Lo que cae antes de la descarga en la terminal
cuando se destraba la boquilla para que caiga
la pastilla interdicta de la purga del gorgojo
más lo que cae entre los listones mal ajustados
de la madera de la caja cuando salta el camión
a causa de una mala maniobra del conductor
o de los pliegues irregulares hechos por el sol
y el pasar firme de las ruedas sobre el asfalto
es nada si se tiene en cuenta que la carga final
en los buques destinados a Brasil, China o Irán
es más de dos millones quinientas mil toneladas,
pero los chanchos y gallinas del lugar no cavilan
igual, tampoco quienes pernoctan en las casillas
con bloques y chapas levantadas junto a la ruta:
luz alta para los anteojos de Moisés S. Rodríguez
que barre de lado a lado banquina y alquitrán
y con la pala junta tosca, tierra, trigo y embolsa.
Eso no es un elástico doble de cama apoyado
sobre un tronco; es la zaranda con que distingue
lo útil de lo que también es útil pero menos.
Qué piensa mientras con hilo grueso y la aguja
pasando a milímetros de su ojo clava y cose
otra bolsa de cuarenta kilos ya llena, la levanta
y apoya en el montón de la puerta de entrada
bajo el cartel en tiza VENDO TRIGO, desconozco.

---

1 Included in the 2017 German edition, but not the Spanish edition.

MEDITATION ON THE PORT LOADING STATISTICS

What's lost before unloading in the terminal
when they undo the nozzle so as to put in
the forbidden tablet to get rid of weevils,
plus what falls between the badly positioned slats
of the container when the lorry jolts about
because of a poor manoeuvre by the driver
or the irregular ridges made by the sun
and the heavy passage of wheels in the tarmac
is nothing if you bear in mind the final load
in ships destined for Brazil, China or Iran
is more than two and a half million tonnes,
but the pigs and chickens don't wonder about it
all the same, and nor do those who live in the huts
of breeze blocks and corrugated iron by the road:
headlights in the glasses of Moisés S. Rodríguez,
who brushes pavement and tarmac from side to side
and with the shovel gathers earth and wheat, bags them.
That is not a double-elasticated sheet bound
round a trunk; it's the sieve that's used to tell
the useful from the also useful, but less so.
What he is thinking while the thick thread and needle
just millimetres from his eye pierces and sews
another full forty-kilo bag, which he lifts,
then places on the pile by the entrance door
under the sign in chalk WHEAT FOR SALE, I don't know.

CABALLOS EN LA VÍA PÚBLICA

Una reglamentación referida a los horarios
en los que es lícito que un decimonónico caballo
haga resonar sus herrajes en la vía pública, eso
es el poder. Por eso apenas la yunta cansada del sol
sobre la loma asoma arriban los carros al galpón
trayendo en sus cajas botellas, cartones y metales
recolectados a lo largo de una noche cualquiera;
aquellos capaces de distinguir la rentabilidad
en lo que el resto de los vecinos considera inútil
sentados van sobre un tablón con las riendas
en la mano, y por las calles de la ciudad deambulan
en concordancia a un tranco cansino que no sabe
de la urgencia del camión de la empresa de limpieza
al que, democrático, todo todo le da igual.
Los animales conocen su recorrido de memoria.
Salvo en una jornada en la que se ha reunido
más de lo habitual y gravoso es el peso de la carga,
no hace falta recordarles la existencia del alma.

HORSES IN THE PUBLIC HIGHWAY

A regulation governing the hours
during which a nineteenth-century horse
may click its hooves on public highways, that
is power. So the moment that the team
arrives, sun-drained, they get the carts into the store
lifting boxes, of bottles, card, metal
collected in one night or another;
those capable of seeing the value
in what the neighbours consider useless
proceed, seated on a board with the reins
in their hands, and wander the city's streets
in time with a tired tread that knows nothing
of the rush of the cleaning business truck,
which, democratically, doesn't give a damn.
The animals have memorised the route.
Except on a day when more is gathered
than normal and the cargo weighs heavy
they need no reminding of the soul's existence.

FILUM ARTHROPODA, CLASE CRUSTACEA

Un collar de nervios complejo
que tiende a la concentración
y la niega: ganglios por segmento
controlan una parte al margen
de otra y el cerebro, que inerva
ojos, antenas y anténulas bien
podría no estar y no ser problema
salvo que las pinzas seguirían
día a día cerrándose abriéndose
contra lo que sea sin necesidad
ni objetivo preciso: en la cabeza
no hay estímulo sino inhibición.
La corteza compuesta de quitina
no es capa ya que se extiende
hacia dentro, tapiza órganos
y hasta músculos en el andar.
Metafóricamente se la asocia
a un escudo de armas por dureza
y función altamente defensiva,
pero por constitución no crece
y ejerce más tarde o temprano
presión para promover la muda.
La formación de la nueva costra
se da en un tiempo extendido
durante el cual el ejemplar
se vuelve vulnerable al extremo.

PHYLUM ARTHROPODA, CLASS CRUSTACEA

A complex necklace of nerves
that tends to concentration
and negates it: ganglia
control one part alongside
another; the brain, which links nerves
to eyes, antennae, antennules,
could vanish, with no problem
except the pincers would go on
for days closing and opening
on anything, needlessly
and aimlessly: in its head
not stimulus, but constraint.
The shell composed of chitin
is no layer: it extends
inside as well, connects organs,
even muscles for walking.
Metaphor associates it
with a coat of arms for hardness
and highly defensive function
but by nature it doesn't grow
and sooner or later exerts
great pressure to make a move.
Formation of a new shell
requires a long time, in which
the individual becomes
extremely vulnerable.

Para eso habría desarrollado ojos
compuestos, miles de ommatidios
cada uno con un campo visual
particular y una córnea propia,
rabdomas donde cierta agudeza
se pierde a favor de la capacidad
de detectar con gran rapidez
el mínimo movimiento cercano,
no siempre con suficiente eficacia.

So it developed compound eyes,
thousands of ommatidia,
each one with its particular
visual field and cornea,
rhabdoms in which some sharpness
is lost in exchange for the skill
of detecting with great speed
the smallest movement nearby,
not always with efficacy.

HÉCTOR CIOCCHINI OBSERVA DOS VECES
UN MISMO LIBRO DE ESTAMPAS

Cuando en los años '60 contemplaba
las páginas de la edición francesa
de la *Hypnerotomachia Poliphili*
de Francesco Colona, se demoraba
una y otra vez ante el gesto detenido
del pie a punto de dar un paso más
con el que la imagen hace girar
a los jóvenes y doncellas que danzan
tomados de la mano como si fueran
una guirnalda. Más de diez años
después, se abisma en lo más obvio:
el rostro doble de cada bailarín
que exhibe la felicidad de un lado
y el dolor del otro. Obra de Guyon,
bajo la escena se lee el mote TEMPVS.

HÉCTOR CIOCCHINI LOOKS A SECOND TIME AT AN INCUNABLE

When in the '60s he looked through
pages of the French edition
of *Hypnerotomachia Poliphili*
by Francesco Colonna, he paused
time and again at the stilled gesture
of a foot at the point of stepping
with which the image sets spinning
the young men and maidens that dance
holding hands, as if they made up
a garland. Well over ten years
later, he sees the obvious:
the double face of each dancer
which shows happiness on one side,
sadness on the other. By Guyon,
below it stands the motto TEMPVS.

PARA UN ESTUDIO DE LA ECONOMÍA DE EXPORTACIÓN

LA NATURALEZA NO ES UN BANCO

Aunque el haz segado de trigo, a la luz última del día,
asemeje su brillo al que tiene el oro, la Naturaleza
no es un banco, y la flexibilidad de la vara no admite
metáfora económica ninguna, salvo cuando restalla.
Y así las grandes cosechas favorecidas por la lluvia
no alcanzaron allá por mil ocho setenta a amortiguar
el déficit provocado por los importantes empréstitos
firmados en Londres que habían permitido extender
el crédito vacante con el que se había creído pagar
la trilladora a vapor. Se importó para exportar, no
para no importar más. Un año o dos sin nubes a la vista
y la trilladora urgida de algún repuesto, y el número
ingente de la deuda, blancos huesos, seco el junco
del fisco junto al arroyo seco, una escena romántica,
al azar del modélico destino liberal que copia y copia
como la literatura de sus ociosos, mucho, mucho y mal.

TOWARDS A STUDY OF THE EXPORT ECONOMY

NATURE IS NOT A BANK

Although the cut wheat sheaves, in the last of day's light,
seem to shine just like gold, Nature is not a bank,
and the suppleness of the stalk does not permit
economic metaphor, except when it breaks.
And therefore the great harvests favoured by the rain
were not enough in 1870 to amortise
the deficit incurred through significant loans
signed in London that enabled the extension
of vacant credit with which they hoped to purchase
the steam harvester. Importing to export, not
to import more. One or two years without a cloud
and the harvester needing a spare, and the huge
figure of the debt, the white bones, the dried-up reed
of the bank by the dried-up creek, romantic scene,
at the whim of model liberal destiny
that copies and copies like the literature
of its chattering classes, much, much, and badly.

MODIFICACIÓN EN LA ALIMENTACIÓN DE LAS LOCOMOTORAS FABRICADAS EN EUROPA

La máquina fue construida en Inglaterra,
y por eso la boca del combustible sólo admitía,
a paladas servido por el foguista de turno,
el reconocido sabor del carbón Cardiff
embarcado ciego durante millas de océano.
Pero llegó la guerra, una primero y después
otra, y la locomotora debió acostumbrar
a la leña el paladar, luego al maíz y al trigo.
Mismo el mecanismo: astillas, empapada estopa
de kerosén, fuego hasta la lámina de agua
que circunda el cielo del horno, fuerza y presión
del vapor acumulado en la caldera, arrojado
sobre los émbolos en los cilindros que lleva
sobre el liso riel dinámica a la rueda, que gira.
Pero la llama no era la misma y ascendía
por la chimenea el humo y una embriaguez
conocida se apoderaba de las aves del lugar
que volaban y parecían acompañar en torno
y numerosas, irregulares la marcha regular.

MODIFICATION TO THE FUEL OF LOCOMOTIVES BUILT IN EUROPE

The engine was constructed in England
and so the fire door only permitted
shovel servings from the on-shift fireman
with the recognized taste of Cardiff coal
shipped in pitch dark across miles of ocean.
But afterwards war came, first one and then
another; the engine had to get used
to wood on its palate, then corn and wheat.
The mechanism's the same: splinters, oakum steeped
in kerosene, flames up to the sheet of water
surrounding the firebox roof, the force and pressure
of steam accumulating in the boiler thrown
onto the pistons in the cylinders and moved
down the smooth dynamic rod to the wheel, which turns.
But the flame was not the same, and so when
the smoke rose from the chimney a well-known
intoxication seized the birds, who flew
in numbers, seeming to accompany,
irregularly, the regular march.

SERGIO RAIMONDI: SELECTED POEMS

LEXIKÓN

LEXIKON

अनयिमतिता

Aun con la súper-computadora de modelado 3D
anunciada por el Ministerio de Ciencias de la Tierra
el fenómeno inconstante del monzón del verano

capaz de traer las lluvias esperadas o la seca fatal
será más fácil de predecir que el hábito recóndito
frecuente entre agricultores del oeste y del sur

de beber el herbicida como si fuera exquisito ron
ante un campo pleno en mijo de cotización baja.
Porque no es la reversión estacional de frío y calor

entre el subcontinente y el océano lo que afecta
el ánimo de quien de pronto se para a contemplar
las ramas demasiado flexibles del árbol de mango

sino la variabilidad bien planificada del proyecto
de transformar una cultura históricamente rural
en una nación urbana, tecnológica y hasta digital

desde el ejemplo exacto que ofrece la modificación
precisa y veloz de un gen en la semilla de algodón.
Se supone que quienes eligen la forma inmolatoria

evalúan soportar el dolor para ofrecer un mensaje
hasta el momento sin una decodificación certera
en la imagen inolvidable de unas llamas a la carrera.

अनियमितता

Even with the 3d-modelling supercomputer
that has been announced by the Ministry of Earth Sciences
the inconstant phenomenon of the summer monsoon

capable of bringing the longed-for rain or lethal drought
will be simpler to predict than the recondite habit
commonly found among the western or southern farmers

of drinking herbicide as if it were exquisite rum
faced with fields full of millet whose price has fallen.
Because it's not the seasonal changes of hot and cold

between the subcontinent and the ocean that affect
the spirit of one who suddenly stops to contemplate
the overly flexible branches of the mango tree

but the well-planned variability of the project
of transforming a historically rural culture
to a nation urban, technological, digital

based on the exact example of modification,
precise and swift, of a gene of the cotton family.
You'd imagine that the ones who choose self-immolation

think it's worth enduring the pain to offer a message
that so far doesn't seem to carry clear meaning
in the unforgettable image of flames on the run.

AUTOR (ALS PRODUZENT, DER)

La época no nos exige espíritu, camaradas
del Instituto para el Estudio del Fascismo:
nos exige movimientos del diafragma.
Por eso les traigo un ejemplo concreto
(¡hoy los ejemplos concretos son rusos!)
de lo que es una obra literaria y política-
mente correcta. Ahí lo tienen a Tretiakov.
¿Cómo escribe el camarada Tretiakov?
Está en las reuniones directivas del koljós
organiza colectas para el pago de tractores
pregunta por acá y por allá para averiguar
cuáles son las mejores colleras y bujías
explica las tesis de Yakovlev y ahora calma
a las madres que se pelean en la guardería
obtiene caballos para el viaje de los maestros
inspecciona los clubes de lectura y envía
tres, diez y cuántas cartas sean necesarias
para exigir el arribo del cine ambulante
documenta con minucia siembra y cosecha
clak clak con su cámara en todos lados.
Sí, también escribe y publica informes
de lo hecho en los periódicos de Moscú
y dirige el diario comunal con información
sobre cómo preparar la tierra y las actividades
previstas para el aniversario de la revolución.

AUTOR (ALS PRODUZENT, DER)

The times don't demand our spirits, comrades
of the Institute for Study of Fascism:
they demand movements of the diaphragm.
So I bring you a concrete example
(today's concrete examples are Russian!)
both a work of literature and poli-
tically correct. Here you have Tretiakov.
How does our Comrade Tretiakov write?
He attends Kolhoz committee meetings
organizes collections for tractors,
he makes enquiries so as to find out
which are the best horse collars, best sparkplugs,
explains Yakovlev's thesis, and now calms
the mothers fighting in the nursery,
obtains horses for the teachers' travel,
inspects the reading clubs and dispatches
three, ten, as many letters as needed
to gain a visit from the mobile cinema,
minutely records sowing and reaping
click click with his camera everywhere.
Yes, and he writes and publishes reports
of what's done in the Moscow newspapers,
edits the community bulletin
on tilling the earth and activities
planned for the Revolution's anniversary.

¿Cómo? No oí bien. ¿Que qué tiene todo esto
que ver con la literatura? Ah, la literatura…
Pero camaradas, ¿son capaces de entender
que el mundo puede cambiar, es más: luchan
día a día para que efectivamente cambie
y exigen una literatura siempre igual a sí misma?

What's that? I didn't hear it. What's all this
to do with literature? Oh, literature…
But, comrades, you're able to understand
that the world can change, and more: you struggle
day after day for it to change, and yet
you demand literature that stays the same?

标签

Si bien en la carrera por la inteligencia artificial
el nivel del desarrollo científico norteamericano

constituye testimonio irrebatible de liderazgo
sería artificial y poco inteligente desestimar

tanto el tamaño excepcional del mercado chino
como su costumbre diaria de utilizar el software

para todo tipo de pagos y trámites bancarios
al punto de transformar los billetes en un objeto

adecuado para el álbum metódico del coleccionista
o para la vitrina de un museo de la vida cotidiana

generando con cada uno de esos movimientos
un volumen ingente de información invalorable

no, tan valuada que hoy puede ser más rentable
iniciar una fábrica de procesamiento de datos

que una empresa para la construcción de viviendas;
así de hecho lo muestran las hileras de hijos únicos

sentados frente a las pantallas y etiquetando
semáforos, rostros, ojos singulares, labios, etc.

标签

Even though in the artificial intelligence race
scientific development in North America

is undeniable testimony of leadership
it would be artificial and unintelligent

to underestimate the huge size of China's market
and the daily custom of employing software

for every kind of payment and banking transfer
almost to the point of turning banknotes into objects

only fit for the methodical album of a collector
or glass cases of a museum of daily life

generating with each of these monetary movements
a vast volume of invaluable information

no, so valued that today it is more profitable
to establish a factory for processing data

than to set up a company for constructing houses
and in fact it can be seen in the lines of only sons

seated in front of computer screens endlessly tagging
traffic lights and faces, odd eyes and lips, etc.

provistos por cámaras y sensores omnipresentes
en el edificio que hasta ayer fuera una cementera

y en cuya entrada yace una mezcladora, signo
físico de un sentido obsoleto de infraestructura.

supplied with omnipresent cameras and sensors
in a building that up until yesterday was a cement works

and in whose entrance sits a mixer, physical
symbol of an obsolete meaning of infrastructure.

BLAKE, WILLIAM

Si quien llegara al muelle de Puerto Piojo
y más allá en todo sentido de las lanchas
que retornan de quién sabe qué riacho
pero en principio en la acepción acotada
que involucra la distancia en el espacio,
viera el más que extenso galpón de Cargill
y tuviera que volver a verlo para advertir
que hoy es inclusive más extenso que ayer,
no fuera un empleado municipal dormido
sino un vate capaz de percibir el porvenir
y seguir sin inconveniente una dinámica
que escapa al resto de los simples mortales,
vería... ¿Qué vería? ¿Con qué lengua vería
lo que vería? ¿Vería también esa lengua
que ha de venir? ¿Y cómo podría comunicar
lo que ha de venir en una lengua futura
sin que su verso se confunda con el timbre
de estas gaviotas que sin parar de girar
chillan como presas de extremo desvarío?

BLAKE, WILLIAM

If someone were to arrive at the wharf
in Puerto Piojo, in every sense
beyond the boats returning from who knows what stream
but primarily in the narrow sense
meaning distance in space, were to notice
Cargill's much more than extensive warehouse
and needed to look again to observe
that today it has got even bigger
than it was yesterday, if they were not
a dozing municipal employee
but a bard able to see the future
and easily follow a dynamic
that escapes the rest of us dull mortals,
they would see... What would they see? In what tongue
would they see what they would see? Would they see
that future language? How would they speak of
what's yet to come in a future language
without their verses mingling with the tones
of these gulls that circling without pause
cry out as if in wild delirium?

BULK-CARRIER

Si bien hay que descontar problemas estructurales
capaces de partir el casco en dos amorosas mitades
de las que fluyen límpidamente diesel y fuel-oil
en las aguas un poco menos límpidas de donde sea

sin olvidar tampoco que el cereal suele asentarse
en cada una de las bodegas iniciada la travesía
y dispensado de sujeción puede de un lado al otro
desplazarse hasta poner término a la estabilidad

problemas por los cuales los ingenieros ya analizan
la combinación entre corrosión, fatiga del acero
de alta resistencia e inclusive la de una tripulación
turbada entre diez lenguas y de resistencia menor

no hay duda que constituyen un nuevo adelanto
en el dominio de la potencia del orbe natural:
más allá de la medallita en el pecho del engrasador,
estos son océanos menos mistéricos e insondables.

El alargamiento creciente de la eslora evidencia
el aumento de la carga y del comercio mundial,
trayectos por las rutas del planeta ya no más
pautados por señales radiales de baja frecuencia:

BULK-CARRIER

Even if we must discount structural problems
capable of breaking the hull in loving halves
out of which flow, purely, diesel oil and fuel oil
into the slightly less pure seas of wherever

nor forgetting that cereal often settles
within each compartment from the start of the voyage
and without any control can shift side to side
enough to ruin the vessel's stability

challenges that caused engineers to analyse
combinations of corrosion, fatigue in steel
with high resistance and also within a crew
confused with ten languages and less resistance

there's no doubt that it constitutes a new advance
in mastery over the natural world's power:
beyond the little medal on the oiler's chest
these are seas less mysterious and unsoundable.

The endless expansion of the ship's length reflects
the increase in cargo and of global commerce
routes across the planet's highways no longer ruled
by broadcast low-frequency radio signals

son desplazamientos enérgicos de oferta y demanda
imposibles de ser registrados con el mareógrafo
los que organizarán en minutos el próximo trayecto
ignorado hasta el momento por el supuesto capitán

quien se dedica por lo pronto a controlar la carga
abiertas las escotillas a lo largo de la única cubierta
y el tubo telescópico y final por el que descienden
toneladas contadas por hora de trigo, soja o maíz.

Con la precaución de no inhalar polvillo en exceso
es ahí donde hay que aproximarse para verificar
fija la atención en el chorro continuo del granel
la motivación básica del diseño: la concentración.

they're energetic shifts of supply and demand
impossible to record on a tidal chart
that can organise in minutes the next journey
unknown until that point by the supposed captain

who's busy at the moment checking the cargo
the hatches open the length of the single deck
and the telescopic final tube through which pour
tonnes counted by the hour of wheat, soya or maize.

Being careful not to breathe too much of the dust
that's where you have to get in close to verify
attention fixed on the continued flow of bulk
the basic aim of the design: concentration.

CESO

¿Qué significa perder? Significa
que esos términos y sintagmas
pensados discutidos escritos
en artículos libros y panfletos
y por supuesto también gritados
¡Imperialismo! ¡Dependencia!
¡Subdesarrollo! ¡Oligarquía!
¡Tercermundismo! ¡Masas! ¡Proceso
revolucionario! de pronto son
impronunciables en realidad
como si se hablara otra lengua
ya no se pueden escuchar más.

¿Qué significa perder? Significa
que ahí mismo donde se estudiaba
El Capital la policía pasará a estudiar
los antecedentes del estudiante.
Significa que los *Cuadernos del Centro*
de Estudios Socio-Económicos
ya no se iniciarán con una cita
de un poeta llamado Javier Heraud.
Significa que vuelve el empirismo.
Significa que el ensayo se suplanta
con el informe a término entregado.
Significa el retorno de la objetividad.

CESO

What does it mean to lose? It means
that those terms and syntagms
those thoughts discussions those writings
in articles books and pamphlets
and of course also shouted out
Imperialism! Dependence!
Underdevelopment! Masses!
Third-Worldism! Oligarchy!
Revolutionary Process! are at once
unspeakable in the real world
as if in another language
that cannot now be heard.

What does it mean to lose? It means
that right there where they once studied
Das Kapital police study
the student's criminal record.
It means that the *Journal of the Centre
of Socio-Economic Studies*
no longer opens with a quote
from the poet Javier Heraud.
It means empiricism has returned.
It means the essay is replaced
with the report turned in on time.
It means objectivity has returned.

CLINKER

Tal como corresponde la nodriza es un contorno oscuro,
más oscuro aún frente al firmamento destinado a exhibir
la sensibilidad exquisita en el empleo de los pigmentos,
pero no fue ese el problema ante "Juliet and her nurse"
obra en la que el romántico J. M. William Turner presenta
en una terraza en el margen derecho e inferior del lienzo
a la amante gentil que apoya, tal como indican los versos,
su mejilla en su mano. Se señaló en cambio la incorrección
de trasladar la escena de la consabida Verona a Venecia
tal vez sin entender que la verdad ofrecida por el gran arte
está más allá de las contingencias de tiempo y espacio.
Antes de embolsar los cincuenta kilos de cemento portland
el polvo en el que se ha convertido la piedra caliza triturada
arriba al silo de homogeneización conformado por un cilindro
extenso e inclinado de acero girando sin cesar sobre rodillos
con temperaturas extremas en aumento de forma gradual
para así calcinar en forma pareja la harina desde el hueco
de entrada al hueco de salida por donde sale ya convertida
en el clinker almacenado tras su enfriamiento en parrillas.
No obstante el proceso laboral se inicia antes en el yacimiento
donde las sombras del técnico y los operarios crean frentes
en la cantera mediante explosiones más o menos controladas
que se remontan a los orígenes de la empresa Loma Negra
fundada en la ciudad de Olavarría por don Alfredo Fortabat
y cuyo patrimonio fue triplicado por su heredera universal
compradora ayer de la obra mencionada al inicio del poema

CLINKER

As is fitting the nurse appears as a shadowy shape
even darker still before the sky whose fate is to show
exquisite sensibility in the use of pigments,
but that was not the problem with 'Juliet and her Nurse'
in which the Romantic J. M. William Turner shows
on a terrace on the right bottom edge of the canvas
the gentle lover who supports, as the lines indicate,
her cheek upon her hand. No, they pointed to the error
of shifting scene from the well-known Verona to Venice
perhaps without understanding that the truth of great art
reaches beyond all the contingencies of time and space.
Before bagging the 50 kilos of Portland cement
the dust into which the crushed limestone has been converted
arrives at the cylindrical homogenisation silo
whose steel length, at an angle, turns endlessly on rollers
with extreme temperatures rising gradually
to calcinate raw meal consistently from entry pipe
to the cooler chute, from which it emerges now transformed
into the clinker that's stored after its cooling on grates.
However, the process starts before in the deposit
where the technician and operators' shadows create
quarry fronts by means of more or less controlled explosions
that go right back to the origins of Loma Negra
founded in Olavarría by Don Alfredo Fortabat
and whose estate has been tripled by his sole heir
buyer yesterday of the work named at this poem's start

en años de desgravaciones impositivas y aumento del dólar.
Esta atención hacia los accidentes se podría recomendar
a los especialistas que todavía hoy debaten la significación
de los cohetes anacrónicos situados en la bóveda, signo avieso
en definitiva, de superar el silencio forzoso de la pintura.

during the years of tax relief and the dollar rising.
This attention to accidents could be recommended
to the specialists that to this day debate the meaning
of anachronistic rockets in the vault, for certain
a perverse sign of overcoming painting's forced silence.

DUAS CIVITATES

A quienes desprecian la existencia de la ciudad celestial
en nombre de la materialidad sospechosa de este mundo
privilegiando el placer de sentidos falibles como el tacto
y las consecuencias del efecto de un abrazo en el cuerpo
desde la alegría acotada que brinda el habitar esta tierra
compartiendo el desinterés por el afán de transcendencia
con la pluralidad variada de los seres vegetales reptileanos
volátiles natátiles ambulátiles es decir irracionales... A ver:
ciertos gusanos capaces de agitarse en el agua que hierve
les han de mostrar qué les espera al final de los tiempos.

Pero en verdad en las afirmaciones del Obispo de Hipona
tan involucrado en la urgencia mutable de sus propios días
cuando el acontecimiento de la barbarie servía para exhibir
otra época más en la que nada se sostenía en estabilidad
correspondería reconocer la historia del entrenamiento
que requiere este presente exigente en reclamar la fe
para experimentar la vida en dos ámbitos simultáneos
y vinculados entre sí: uno inmanente fragmentario efímero
otro virtual donde a quienes tienden hacia lo intangible
un Dios triunfal les asegura una vida dichosa y eterna.

DUAS CIVITATES

For those who sneer at the existence of the heavenly city
in the name of the suspect materiality of this world
privileging the pleasure of the fallible senses like touch
and the consequence of the effect of a hug on the body
from the limited joy that derives from inhabiting this earth
sharing disinterest with regard to the desire for transcendence
with the plurality of beings vegetable reptilian
airborne aquatic ambulant that is irrational… Let's see:
some types of worm that are able to wriggle in boiling water
should suffice to show them what is awaiting at the end of times.

But in truth in the affirmations of the Bishop of Hippo
so involved in the mutable urgencies of his own era
when the pressing occurrence of barbarism indicated
yet another epoch in which nothing was to remain stable
it would be correct to recognise the history of practice
that this demanding present moment demands, requiring the faith
to experience life in two dimensions simultaneously
each linked to the other: one ephemeral immanent fragmentary
and one virtual where for those tending towards the intangible
a triumphal God assures them a blissful and eternal life.

ESCALATOR

Cada vez que se aproxima el extremo contrario
    donde los rígidos peldaños acanalados pierden
        la apariencia de su forma y se vuelven cinta

continua lanzada a rehacer la operación otra vez
    según una mecánica capaz de instalar el concepto
        de que cuenta la circulación no un rumbo eventual

de hecho el sentido es reversible y arriba y abajo
    intercambiables mediante un simple dispositivo
        pasible de fallar sin embargo ante el uso frecuente

convendría no voy a decir detenerse a reflexionar
    no se trata de favorecer el riesgo de un accidente
        pero sí reflexionar desde ese movimiento aparente

sobre la relación entre el devenir de las sustancias
    y el de las compañías, reconversión de un rinde
        en desplazamiento constante a lo largo del planeta

aleación ayer usada para dejar en el aire vestigios
    explosivos de una munición de cañón de sesenta mm
        del otro lado del mundo y que ahora en el descanso

inicial, final y ambiguo de esta escalera automática
    indica el pasaje de un paradigma de la guerra a otro:
        fusión figurada THYSSENKRUPP en el acero fundido.

ESCALATOR

Every time it approaches the far end
    the rigid steps discard the appearance
        of their form and instead become a belt

endlessly in the same operation
    via a mechanism that asserts
        circulation counts, not destination:

it is reversible, with up or down
    interchanged using a simple device
        that, however, may fail if overused.

It is worth, I will say, not reflecting
    on the likelihood of an accident
        but thinking from this apparent movement

to what links the development of substances
    and that of companies, reworking a return
        into constant displacement across the planet

of an alloy once used to leave airborne traces
    of a 60mm shell's explosives
        from the far side of the world now seeming at rest

at the start or finish of this automatic stairway
    marking the slip from a war footing to another kind:
        a fusion written THYSSENKRUPP into the cast steel base.

FISH BLOCK

Porque por supuesto aun la misma fluidez del pez en el agua
a ver, más específicamente: ese vértice agudo y extendido
de la merluza de cola magallánica útil para moverse en orden
múltiple a cien dos tres cuatrocientos metros de profundidad
vuelta otra vez a las capas altas del Atlántico y Pacífico sur
ha de terminar compactada solidificada congelada embalada
para asumir así la forma vigente de la producción industrial

paralelogramo premium de siete kilos y medio de filet de hoki
medida estandarizada y universal de la lengua y las máquinas
comercio y transporte a través de paralelogramos semejantes
ángulos sin imperfecciones y una superficie alisada de vacío
exacta para diluir los movimientos de la mano que evisceria
extrae el epitelio y se dispone ya a realizar el despinado fino
a bordo de un arrastrero cuya bandera no importa demasiado.

FISH BLOCK

Because of course the same fluidity of fish in the water,
well, more specifically: of that sharp and extended vertex
of the Patagonian grenadier that's useful for moving
in multiple order at one, two, three, four hundred metres' depth
has to end up compacted solidified frozen and packaged
to adopt the usual form of industrial production:

premium parallelogram, 7.5 kilos of hoki
the standardised and universal measure of taste and machines
of commerce and transport across similar parallelograms
with angles that lack imperfections, vacuum-smooth surface
exact to dilute the movements of the hand that eviscerates
extracts the epithelium and begins the fine deboning
on a trawler whose flag doesn't matter much.

FOUCAULT, MICHEL

Filósofo e historiador a ver… ¿a qué no adivinan?
francés cuyas obras en torno a los dispositivos
e instituciones de normalización fueron leídas
de este lado del orbe con los regímenes militares
en mente o mejor inscriptos en las coyunturas
óseas y las terminales deterioradas y nerviosas
sin alcanzar a reconocer cómo esa perspectiva
sobre un poder estatal total reticulado panóptico
disciplinario etc fue elaborada desde el seminario
de un colegio nacional anteayer imperial sostenido
por políticas públicas no paradójicamente potentes;
lo paradójico fue tal vez demorarse en los planos
arquitectónicos de Bentham y sus correspondencias
subjetivas mientras el Estado local era evacuado
sin advertir una no muy sutil diferencia cualitativa:
que acá el infante sea conducido a la escuela barrial
donde se le corrija el hábito malsano de pretender
escribir en un pupitre normal con la mano siniestra
y efectivamente encuentre en principio un pupitre,
un cuaderno y una escuela además de, por supuesto,
el docente coercitivo y más o menos mal pago
tal vez no sea un hecho tan merecedor de desprecio.

FOUCAULT, MICHEL

Philosopher and historian let's see … can you guess?
A Frenchman whose writings concerning the apparatus
and the institutions of normalisation were read
over this side of the orb with military regimes
in mind or rather inscribed into the joints between bones
and our worn, nervous terminals without ever recognising
how this perspective on a state's power as a network
total panoptical disciplinary etc.
was thought from a seminar at a once imperial
national college not long since sustained by public policies
unparadoxically powerful; the paradox
was perhaps to pause over Benthamite architecture's
subjective correspondences while the state was hollowed
without seeing one unsubtle qualitative difference:
the child taken to the neighbourhood school where they correct
his unhealthy habit of writing at a normal desk
with his left hand and effectively finding for the first time
a desk an exercise book a school as well as, of course,
the coercive teacher who is more or less badly paid
perhaps may prove to be a fact less worthy of disdain.

GLOMEROMYCETES

La posibilidad de ver
del siglo pasado
o sea endomicorrizas
para recibir azúcar
y brindar a cambio

menos un fenómeno
que una asociación
entre dos organismos
y el despliegue inicial

no hay que rastrearla
y las colaboraciones
sino mejor en el éxito
del Estado de Bienestar
cumplida por entonces

decididos en conjuntos
las ideas extendidas
proyectadas sin cesar
como si ahí solo hubiera

recién en la mitad
en las hifas fúngicas
penetrando la raíz
de la fotosíntesis
fósforo y nitrógeno

patógeno o parásito
simbiótica o mutual
a remitir al Ordovícico
de plantas en la tierra

en el avance científico
entre biólogos diversos
temporal y acotado
y la función decisiva
por sindicatos y gremios

a apaciguar y revertir
del libre mercado
en la naturaleza misma
competencia letal

GLOMEROMYCETES

The possibility
through the past century
or endomicrosomes
to receive the sugar
and offer in return

of seeing just halfway
in the fungal filaments
penetrating the root
of photosynthesis
phosphorus, nitrogen

less something parasitic
than an association
between two organisms
and the first dispersion

or pathological
symbiotic or mutual
since the Ordovician
of plants across the earth:

there's no need to trace it
and the collaboration
rather in the success
achieved by the Welfare State
syndicates and unions

in science's advance
among biologists
temporal and constrained
and the decisive role
played in this period

committed together
the developed ideas
projected without cease
as if it only involved

to pacify and reverse
about the free market
as nature itself
deadly competition

GOLD EXCHANGE STANDARD

Pero entonces el filósofo no debería continuar buscando
la memoria rítmica de una lengua perdida en la lengua
invocar el verso hermético de un trovador del siglo doce
o reconocer en la parataxis de ése malherido por el rayo
la voluntad de ir más allá de lo comunicativo liberando
al ónoma de la trama insoportable del blableo discursivo

porque siempre y cuando tengamos en cuenta la relación
íntima entre la acuñación de las monedas y las palabras
habría sido acaso un acto presidencial y ¡performático!
equivalente a la destrucción mosaica del becerro idolátrico
la que consiguió cumplir así el sueño perfecto de decir
literalmente nada al desvincular dólar y lingote de oro

GOLD EXCHANGE STANDARD

So then the philosopher should not continue to seek
the rhythmic memory of a lost language in language
invoking a 12th-century troubadour's hermetic verse
or see in the parataxis of one hurt by lightning
a will to surpass the communicative by freeing
the onoma from the unbearable weft of blah blah

since whenever we take into account the intimate
relation between the striking of the coin and the words
we would see an act presidential – and performative! –
equivalent to Moses destroying the idolatrous calf
which succeeded in realising the perfect dream of saying
literally nothing in uncoupling dollar and ingot of gold

HADESARCHEA

El sol nunca existió.
No, nunca ese disco
único central real
destinado a limitar
las formas existentes
anunció su dominio
acá en lo profundo.
Qué liberación. Esta
bacteria extremófila
con su metabolismo
flexible y heredado
capaz de transformar
con quimiosíntesis
el dióxido de carbono
en materia orgánica
y fuente de energía
tiene en su genoma
inscripta la memoria
negada: la oscuridad
también enseña a vivir.

HADESARCHAEA

The sun never was.
No, never did that disc
unique central real
destined to limit
the forms that exist
announce dominion
down here in the deep.
What liberation. This
extremophile cell
its metabolism
inherited agile
able to transform
through chemosynthesis
carbon dioxide
to organic matter
a source of energy
has in its genome
inscribed negated
memory: darkness
also teaches living.

灰色气体

De la conciencia surgida del desarrollo tecnológico ulterior
emanan ahora sentidos oscuros, infectos, en fin, negativos
sobre el combustible sostén de toda la industria primera

aunque en este estricto presente y en la República Popular
millones se hundan para extraerlo medio kilómetro bajo tierra
acarrearlo luego en la mitad de los vagones disponibles y al fin

secar los ajíes en el hornillo, fundir acero, producir electricidad.
Es innegable que son seis mil los casos anuales por fuga de gas
o por el agua que, en minutos, sumerge el fondo del socavón,

pero ante volúmenes extralimitados de todo (territorio, historia,
marchas, murallas) cabe entender que el pensar decisivo
de los miembros del comité permanente del Buró del Partido

se tenga que adecuar al orbe definitivo de las estadísticas
para concebir esas muertes sin duda más que lamentables
como parte de la política demográfica y la planificación familiar.

灰色气体

From the knowledge learned through subsequent technological
    development
there now emanate dark meanings, infected, in summary, negative,
about the combustible fuel that sustains all primary industry

although in this narrow present and in the People's Republic many
millions bury themselves to extract it half a kilometre below ground
and then cart it in half the available wagons and at last

dry off chillies on the stove, or forge steel, or produce electricity.
It's undeniable that there are six thousand cases each year
    from gas leaks
or from flooding that, in minutes, submerges the whole depth
    of the tunnel,

but faced with endless volumes of everything (territory, history,
marches, murals) it is necessary to grasp that the decisive thought
of the members of the permanent committee of the Party Bureau

has to operate definitively within the realm of statistics
to conceptualise these deaths that are without doubt more
    than lamentable
as a part of their demographic policy and family planning.

ID BLOCK

Aunque la teoría algorítmica de la información no será útil
para comprobar si el aumento exponencial de la velocidad
de los procesamientos medidos en exahashes por segundo
con el fin de desencriptar las codificaciones más complejas
y permitir seguir así creando en cada nodo la moneda digital

está en correspondencia con el nivel también exponencial
de la anacronía que va adquiriendo la autoridad histórica
monopólicamente a cargo de su emisión control y circulación
incluyendo el vínculo clásico entre centralismo y soberanía
o problemáticas jurisdiccionales en otro tiempo decisivas.

ID BLOCK

Although algorithmic information theory won't help
to tell if the exponential rise in velocity
of processing measured in exahashes per second
with the aim of decrypting the most complex encodings
to permit creation in each node of digital coins

is in accord with the similarly exponential level
of anachronism historic authority gains
a monopoly on emission control and circulation
including centralism and sovereignty's classic bonds
or jurisdictional questions in past times decisive.

INNGERIS

Numerosas razones en su mente de estadista
el padre fundador de la nación singapurense

formado en Cambridge sopesó al promulgar
la paradójica independencia en inglés oficial:

disponer de una dicción equitativa y distante
para favorecer la comunicación entre etnias

y sus voces diversas en mandarín, en malayo
y el tamil de los migrantes del sur de la India;

aprovechar el aparato administrativo recibido
sin necesidad de ponerse a traducir pilas y pilas

de decretos y leyes en medio de otros asuntos
de carácter tal vez un poco más urgente;

y reconocer que la chance de hacer de la ínsula
un enclave comercial, tecnológico y financiero

dependía al final de la infraestructura básica
tiempo atrás levantada bajo órdenes británicas:

no los diques destinados a sofrenar las mareas
y los primeros muelles agitados de lo que es hoy

INNGERIS

The statesman's mind possessed by the founding father
of the nation of Singapore (formed in Cambridge)

weighed many reasons for paradoxically
phrasing independence in official English:

to have a diction equitable and distant
favouring communication of ethnic groups

and their diverse voices in Mandarin, Malay
and the Tamil of migrants from south India;

to employ the inherited bureaucracy
without the need to be translating piles and piles

of decrees and law in the midst of other tasks
whose character was perhaps more urgent;

to see the chance to make the island an enclave
commercial, technological and financial

rested in the end on basic infrastructure
previously built on the orders of the British:

not the dams that were designed to hold back the tides
and the first harbour walls raised from what is today

pasaje clave entre unas aguas oceánicas y otras
uno de los puertos más estratégicos del planeta

sino el idioma mismo, habla global de compras
y ventas y tantos términos de trámites bancarios.

a key passage from one ocean to another
one of the most strategic ports on the planet

but language itself, global speech of purchases
and sales and so many terms for bank transactions.

INTERNACIONAL, LA

No, "Peones del mundo uníos" no
da, no dio. Difícil imaginar el grito
sino solitario y en medio del trigal,
la charla estratégica para planear
la revuelta entre cinco paisanos
bajo la noche vacía y más extensa
con la antorcha libertaria mutada
en fogata para achuras y chorizos
y el relato en torno a una luz mala
poco menos natural que el patrón.
Imposible la Internacional devenida
milonga y la llegada clandestina
a qué buzón de qué tranquera
de la propaganda más disolvente
con el rebelde leyendo *El Capital*
ahí bajo el ombú y los plastones
rumiantes todo alrededor. Cuanto
más para la cosecha advenedizos
o directamente crotos anarquistas
en cualquier poblado de La Pampa
dispuestos a desajustar en silencio
–mientras se ven entre eucaliptus
los faros de la furgoneta policial–
tuercas y tornillos de la John Deere.
Pero la cosecha ya se terminó.
A la hora de roturar, de dar vuelta
todo, otra vez solo ocho, diez.

INTERNACIONAL, LA

No, 'Peons of the world unite', no way,
never. It's hard to imagine the cry
except alone in the middle of wheat fields,
the strategic chat to plan the revolt
with just five peasants in the empty night
widened with the torch of liberty turned
into a fire for offal and sausage
and the tales told around a sickly light
just barely less natural than the boss.
Impossible *The International* turned
tango, and the clandestine arrival
into what postbox hanging on what gate
of the most subversive propaganda
with the rebel reading *Das Kapital*
there under the ombú tree surrounded
by the lumpy ruminants. All the more
for the newly arrived harvest workers
or directly anarchistic hobos
in whichever village in La Pampa
who are disposed to loosen in silence
– while you can see through the eucalyptus
police van lights – the John Deere's nuts and screws.
But the harvest is already finished.
At the ploughing time, for overturning
everything, there are only eight or ten.

IPA

Quizá no sea una ocurrencia ocurrente
justo ahora en medio de los festejos
al borde de la pinta acercar la nariz
para notar en los aromas del lúpulo
responsable de la palidez amarga
característica peculiar de este sabor
la solución para que toneles y toneles
en las embarcaciones ya descargadas
de algodón o fina seda se cargaran
en el muelle ribereño de la compañía
monopólica de la nación propagadora
de la concepción del libre comercio
soportaran el trayecto de seis meses
tras atravesar el ecuador matemático
y lentos circunvalar el cabo africano
entre elevadas temperaturas y olas
que de un lado al otro los desplazaban
llegaran al puerto populoso de Madrás
y en las gargantas resecas terminaran
no de la desinteresada población local
sino de los burócratas civiles y oficiales
del ejército del imperio atareados
día a día en jugar al tenis o disparar
sobre un elefante legendario sentados
para hacer una concesión al exotismo
tigres surgidos de pronto entre tecas

IPA

Perhaps not an occurring occurrence
just now in the midst of festivities
to bring the nose in closer to the pint
to observe in the aroma of hops
responsible for the bitter paleness
peculiar aspect of this flavour
the answer that meant barrels and barrels
in the embarkations once unloaded
of cotton or silk would be loaded
on the riverside wharf of the monopoly
of the nation that first propagated
the ideology around free trade
would endure for the journey of six months
via the mathematical equator
circumnavigating Africa's cape
among the high temperatures and waves
that rolled them from one side to the other,
would land at the crowded port of Madras
and would finish up in the thirsty throats
not of the disinterested locals
but of civil servants and officials
of the imperial army busy
day to day playing tennis or shooting
sat on a legendary elephant
as a concession to the exotic
tigers rushing suddenly from the teaks

y acostumbrar el paladar al curry
o al arroz pilaf con sorbos de esta bebida
hasta volverla tan habitual y necesaria
que décadas después, ya de regreso
en una metrópolis por siempre alterada
hubo gran demanda interna para llenar
la jarra espumosa con que desayunaban
a las tres cuatro de la tarde, aturdidos
ante su color ambivalente y extraño.

and getting the palate used to curry
or pilau rice by sipping from this drink
until the habit's so necessary
that some decades later, having returned
to a metropolis forever changed
there was a great internal need to fill
the foaming glass with which they breakfasted
at three or four in the afternoon, stunned
by its colour ambivalent and strange.

ITO

Tampoco es tanta la diferencia entre tocar una epidermis y tocar
la superficie suave de la pantalla. Con cada ejercitación diaria
se añade otra sensibilidad en la zona de la yema de los dedos
hábiles para detectar en su pasaje sobre la capa de electrodos
la inconveniencia de diferenciar entre lo material e inmaterial.

Pero si la liberación de la locomoción tuvo sus consecuencias
en la conformación paciente de las circunvoluciones del cerebro
obvio que estos roces han de implicar un modo nuevo de pensar
a inscribirse en músculos que retienen aun la inervación agitada
de las aletas de los primitivos elasmobranquios bajo el océano.

ITO

Neither is there so much difference between touching skin
   and touching
the smooth surface of the screen. With every daily interaction
you gain more sensitivity in the zones of the fingertips
skilled in detecting during their passage over the electrodes
the inconvenience of telling material from immaterial.

But if the liberation of movement had its consequences
in patient elaboration of the brain's circumvolutions
it's obvious that these touches must imply a new way of thinking
to be marked in muscles that retain the busy innervation
of the fins of primitive elasmobranchs beneath the ocean.

KEPLERBAHN

El acontecimiento no consiste en permutar la tierra
por un sol: qué cambia si el centro se mantiene.
El problema de calcular la órbita de ese astro rojo
aprovechando las mediciones de la meticulosidad
tenía que ver con el peso de una idea preconcebida
o más bien con el prejuicio griego por comprender
la totalidad más perfecta y unitaria según la esfera.

Solo una verificación matemática había permitido
soportar de pronto el escándalo de la deformación.
Pero una ecuación decimoséxtica no suele impedir
que el sentido insista en decir lo mismo cada vez
y entonces las estrellas pueden persistir en su pasar
circular, terso y regular hasta el fin de los tiempos
distraídas de las posibilidades de la excentricidad.

KEPLERBAHN

What's happening does not consist in permuting the earth
with a sun: what changes if the centre remains steady.
The difficulty calculating that red star's orbit
though taking advantage of meticulous measurement
was to do with the weight of a preconceived idea
or rather with the Greek prejudice for comprehending
the most perfect unified totality as the sphere.

Only mathematical verification allowed
tolerance of the sudden scandal of deformation.
But a sixteenth-century equation rarely impedes
the senses from insisting on saying the same each time
meaning therefore the stars can persist with their circular
passage, terse and regular up until the end of time
distracted from the potential of eccentricity.

KEYWORDS

Comprender las distintas clases de sentido
del término clase no contribuye demasiado
a resolver de una vez las disputas clasistas,
pero abandonar el lenguaje a especialistas
puede ser temerario si existe la pretensión
de encarar una estrategia radical y política:
pensar la lengua es pensar las comunidades
posibles, cambiantes y siempre en tensión
como la misma lengua que al final ¿qué es?
Un modo de producir el mundo y habitarlo.
Es improbable salir urgido de la asamblea
para ir a encontrar el examen impersonal
de un término debatido en ese diccionario
oxoniano y monumental. Más improbable
es encontrar ahí cualquier impersonalidad
y no la perspectiva conservadora y erudita
de sus decimonónicamente sabios editores.
Quien se dedicó a inspeccionar los sentidos
varios y conflictivos de un vocabulario clave
lo consultaba de hecho en su vida militante
para reconocer cómo el significado admitía
la deriva material de las transformaciones,
pero en la biblioteca de su casa no brillaba,
signo propio de la cultura como ostentación,
la letra dorada de los tomos encuadernados:
regalo de un alumno de sus clases de adultos

KEYWORDS

Understanding the distinct classes of meaning
of the term class does not contribute all that much
to finally resolving disputes about class
but to abandon the language to specialists
can be risky if the intention to deal with
radical political strategy exists:
thought about words is thought about communities
those possible, changing and always in tension
with the very language that in the end is what?
A way of producing and living in the world.
It's unlikely you'd rush away from the rally
to find the impersonal examination
of a debated term in that monumental
Oxonian dictionary. More unlikely
still to find there any impersonality,
not the conservative, erudite perspective
of its editors' nineteenth-century wisdom.
He who set himself to inspecting the meanings
various and conflicting of essential terms
consulted it in his life as a militant
and therefore recognised how the sense admitted
the material drift of the transformations
but in his house's library there was no shine,
diagnostic mark of ostentatious culture,
on the golden lettering of the bound volumes:
a gift from a pupil in his adult classes

quien los había comprado semana a semana,
los fascículos con los títulos "R to reactive"
estaban en tres cajas inmensas de cartón:
esas páginas ya no tenían tersura ninguna,
y la tonalidad amarilla del paso del tiempo
era recordatorio de que la fuerza del cambio
estaba en las hablas no registradas, diarias
y populares en las que el presente ordinario
con conciencia, o ni tanto, templa la historia.

who had bought them one by one week by week,
the volumes with their titles 'R to reactive'
were contained in three enormous cardboard boxes:
those pages had by now lost all of their smoothness
and the yellow tone marking the passage of time
was a reminder about how the force of change
was in unrecorded utterances, daily,
popular, in which the ordinary present
consciously, or not so much, tempers history.

ເຂົ້າ

Dado que las ocho mil variedades cultivadas en Laos
uno de los países menos desarrollados del planeta
tanto en el valle del Mekong como en las tierras altas

donde una familia de campesinos habría escuchado
a ancianos de la generación anterior que a su vez
habrían escuchado a otros sabios anteayer ancianos

sobre las ventajas de sembrar cinco granos diferentes
en terrazas diversas a fin de reducir riesgos y distribuir
mejor las actividades entre los miembros de la casa

se hallan en condiciones excelentes de conservación
en un banco genético internacional encargado de suplir
unas mismas semillas intervenidas de rendimiento

superior que permitan la reinversión en fertilizantes
sistemas de riego aptos para mitigar la sinrazón pluvial
y tractores que reemplacen al búfalo senil de la parcela

esta apertura económica es una oportunidad exacta
para lamentar líricamente con un dolor subjetivo
intenso y por supuesto (¿cómo si no?) figurado

la pérdida inminente de una cultura milenaria más.

ເຊົາ

Given that the eight thousand cultivated types in Laos
one of the least developed countries on the planet
the same in the Mekong Valley as up in the highlands

where a family of peasants would have listened
to those of an older generation who in their turn
would have listened to the older wise ones of yesteryear

speak on the advantages of sowing five distinct grains
in different terraces to reduce risks and distribute
better all the tasks among the members of the household

are found in excellent conditions of conservation
in an international gene bank that's charged with supplying
the same seeds, performance genetically modified,

improved to permit reinvestment in fertilisers
irrigation to mitigate the pluvial madness
tractors to replace the senile buffalo on the plot

this economic opening is the precise moment
to lament lyrically and with a subjective woe
that's intense and of course (how otherwise?) figurative

the looming loss of one more millennia-old culture.

ЛАЦИС , АННА

¿O sea que Rusia muestra al mundo el futuro
y Ud. se dedica a estudiar obras barrocas
del siglo diecisiete que nadie sino Ud. mismo
tiene la parsimonia suficiente para leer?
La observación crítica no provenía de un cuerpo
teórico distinto sino de uno concreto y apoyado
contra la mesada de la cocina del departamento.
Blblblblbl. El agua para los spaghetti ya hervía.
No se podía contestar sin percibir la asincronía
radical del intento Bueno, es más complejo
se trata de introducir categorías estéticas útiles
para el análisis del arte más contemporáneo...
No, porque no era solo una pregunta específica;
era además una puesta en duda del alcance
de su pasión en referencia a la vida en general
y en particular a esa historia que comenzaba.
-Se intuían las rodillas bajo el vestido de verano
y el fenómeno bolchevique estaba ahí mismo
con voluntad y decisión para hacer de la filosofía
una praxis cotidiana y constante. ¿No será mucho?
Ah, pasar de revisar incunables en la hemeroteca
a escribir sobre los carteles de la vía pública,
las postales y el diseño de las vidrieras fue entonces
la mayor declaración de amor; insuficiente, obvio.

ЛАЦИС , АННА

So while Russia is showing the world the future
you devote yourself to studying baroque works
of the seventeenth century that none but you
would have sufficient parsimony to read through?
The observation did not come from a distinct
theoretical body but a concrete one
leaning against the kitchen counter in the flat.
Blublub. The water for spaghetti was boiling.
No way to answer without seeing radical
asynchrony of effort Well, it's more complex
to create useful aesthetic categories
for analysis of contemporary art…
No, for it was not just a specific question
it was also a putting in doubt of the reach
of his passion in terms of life in general,
in particular that history he'd started.
You could make out her knees under the summer dress
and the Bolshevik phenomenon was right there
willed and determined to make of philosophy
a daily, constant praxis. Isn't that a lot to ask?
Ah, to go from checking books in the library
to writing about signs on the public highway
postcards and the designs of shop windows was then
love's greatest declaration; not enough, of course.

LAVORO (DOMESTICO)

Porque por supuesto puede suceder que un dato primordial
de una obra monumental cuatro veces redactada y compuesta
por tres volúmenes de trescientas y pico de páginas cada uno
advertencia del traductor prólogo a la primera edición prólogo
a la segunda edición prólogo y epílogo a la edición francesa
prólogo a la tercera edición (alemana) prólogo a la edición inglesa
prólogo a la cuarta edición (alemana) sección sobre mercancía
y dinero sección sobre la transformación del dinero en capital
sección sobre la producción de plusvalor absoluto sección
cuarta sección quinta sección sexta sección séptima y etcétera
se encuentre de repente en la mancha de café en alguna hoja.

LAVORO (DOMESTICO)

Because naturally it can happen that a primordial detail
of a monumental work four times attempted and that's composed
of three volumes each one of slightly more than three hundred pages
translator's commentary prologue to the first edition prologue
to the second edition prologue and epilogue to the French
edition prologue to the third edition (German) prologue
to the English edition prologue to the fourth edition (German)
section on goods and money section on transition of money
into capital section on surplus value production fourth
section fifth section sixth section seventh et cetera
is found suddenly in a coffee stain on one page or other.

ЛК-110Я

Más allá de las alarmas por el futuro del futuro
las temperaturas en aumento en el círculo ártico
que adelgazan día a día témpanos y banquisas
no constituyen necesariamente una mala noticia:

los recursos hidrocarburíferos todavía intocados
y amplísimos se vuelven cada vez más asequibles
las capas rígidas que cubren hasta el horizonte
se debilitan y favorecen el auge de las disputas

por territorios aún en litigio y hasta escándalos
como el de establecer una bandera rusa de titanio
en el fondo mismo de las profundidades marinas
inútil en términos legales pero eficaz para mostrar

una larga historia nacional de inventar estrategias
para embestir sobre el frío literal y metafórico
manifestada ahora en la potencia del rompehielos
que con su casco doble reforzado por una aleación

de cromo níquel molibdeno y vanadio, alto se alza
desde la fuerza de sus dos reactores nucleares
que mueven tres motores de propulsión eléctrica
que hacen girar a su vez a gran velocidad las hélices

ЛК-110Я

Beyond alarm for the future's future
the rising temperatures in the Arctic
that day by day thin out ice packs and floes
don't necessarily equal bad news:

the hydrocarbon reserves yet untouched
and vast each day are more accessible
the block rigid out to the horizon
weakens and favours the rise of disputes

litigation over territories,
scandals, like a metal Russian flag set
right at the bottom of the marine depths
meaningless in law but good for showing

a national history of strategies
for crossing the cold, metaphorical and real,
manifest now in an icebreaker's force
which with its alloy-strengthened double hull

of chrome nickel molybdenum vanadium
surges with its two nuclear reactors
that drive three electric-powered engines
that in turn at speed rotate the propellers

para cumplir nominalista la promesa de su nombre
sobre la mayormente congelada superficie blanca
de la Ruta Marítima del Norte y una estela trazar
con estruendo de hielos rotos limpiando el paso

a fin de que petroleros y gaseros librados del ritmo
en apariencia inevitable de la naturaleza transporten
desde las novísimas plataformas de extracción
ubicadas offshore en el inclemente mar de Kara

sin que importe demasiado el grupo internacional
de activistas preocupados por el repentino derrame
capaz de destruir el hábitat del oso polar la energía
a los puertos de las naciones asiáticas de avanzada.

to keep the nominalist promise of its name
over the mostly frozen white surface
of the Northern Sea Route and trace a wake
the roar of broken ice clearing a way

so oil and gas tankers freed from nature's
apparent inevitable rhythm
can transport from new extraction platforms
located in the hostile Kara Sea

largely ignoring the international
activist group worried by sudden leaks
that might wreck polar bear habitat energy
to the most advanced Asian nations' ports.

LUKÁCS, GYÖRGY

Porque evaluar la pertinencia o no de este verso
es decir por ejemplo de su extensión o del efecto
rítmico ajustado entre sílabas, pausas y acentos
ha de suponer analizar con el mayor detenimiento
el movimiento de aquella grúa-portacontenedores
sobre el hormigón del muelle recién inaugurado
pero a la vez también las eternas leyes genéricas
derivadas de la crítica de la poesía más universal.

¿Cubiertas prendidas fuego en los accesos a puerto?
Abstraer, ya, la cadencia de los versos de Sófocles.
Percibir en esa cadencia una información esencial
necesaria para captar la novedad de esos hechos
– o en todo caso su carácter anacrónico e ineficaz.
Esto no es expresión de una subjetividad exasperada.
Esto es ámbito de una serie objetiva de exigencias
desde donde recusar la segmentación cotidiana.

LUKÁCS, GYÖRGY

Because to assess this line's pertinence or not
that's to say for instance its length or the effect
of rhythm adjusted between syllables, pauses, stress
should suppose analysing with the greatest care
the movement of that container carrier crane
stood on that recently established wharf's concrete
but at once too the eternal laws of genre
drawn from critique of the most universal verse.

Tyres set on fire at the entrances to the port?
To abstract, now, the cadence of Sophocles' lines.
To perceive in that cadence key information
needed to capture the novelty of events
– or at least their anachronistic, useless form.
This is not an exasperated subjectivity.
It is the space of an objective set of conditions
from which to refuse everyday segmentation.

ΝΑΡΘΗΞ

Ahora que el monte Olimpo es una reserva natural
y las decisiones sobre la vida diaria de los mortales

se toman en otras alturas, vítreas y más remotas,
como la asistencia financiera destinada a resolver

el déficit crónico acumulado en años de bárbaro
despilfarro a cambio de medidas de austeridad

consistentes en despidos en los empleos públicos
aumento de impuestos y edad jubilatoria etc.

es entendible que la astucia también se expanda
y las calderas alimentadas con el diesel costoso

poco a poco se apaguen en los meses del invierno
mientras crece la demanda de estufas a alimentar

con zapatos, muebles viejos, nueces y carozos
además de leña obvia comprada en los puestos

ya multiplicados a lo largo y a lo ancho del país
o trozada en el patio de la casa tras hachar

cuanto tronco se pueda encontrar en cercanías
incluidos robles y encinas de aquella reserva divina

ΝΑΡΘΗΞ

Now that Mount Olympus is a nature reserve
and decisions on the daily life of mortals

are taken on other heights, glassy and remote
such as the financial assistance to resolve

the deficit built up through years of barbarous
wastage in exchange for austerity measures

consistent with public sector worker sackings,
raising taxes, retirement age, etc.

it is understandable that such astuteness expands
and the boilers fed with expensive diesel

little by little go out in the winter months
while the demand grows for stoves that can be supplied

with shoes, old furniture, and nuts and pips
in addition obviously to wood bought at stalls

now multiplied the length and breadth of the country
or split in the yard outside after cutting down

whatever trees that could be found growing nearby
including the holm oaks from that divine reserve

serruchados y extraídos por titanes clandestinos
en horas de la noche mientras la policía forestal

con salarios a la baja hace como que los persigue
en el único vehículo aún con nafta en el tanque.

Amparadas en la reciente conciencia ambiental
las autoridades se preocupan hoy por esa nube

gris amarillenta que cubre el cielo de las ciudades:
es el humo ambiguo del retorno de los sacrificios.

sawed up and extracted by clandestine Titans
during nighttime hours while the forestry police

with reduced salaries pretend they're giving chase
in the one truck that's still got petrol in the tank.

Prompted by new environmental awareness
the authorities are worried about that cloud

grey and yellowish that covers the cities' skies:
ambiguous smoke of a return to sacrifice.

MIND UPLOADING

De alcanzarse la tecnología necesaria para transferir
tras escanear las capas microscópicas del cerebro
la mente a un soporte tecnológico o avatar digital
y lograr librarlo así por fin del obstáculo del cuerpo

sería lógico que ese ¿qué? ¿yo? dedicara su tiempo
interminable a hacer unas meditaciones filosóficas
destinadas a mostrar las bondades de dejar afuera
lo incierto y discordante de la razón geométrica:

ese orbe confuso de las impresiones múltiples
provenientes de los sentidos siempre falibles
del oído o el olfato con su tendencia a estremecer
la reflexividad del alma desde el reino de lo extenso.

Pero tal como a aquellos a quienes se les amputa
un brazo o una pierna, también podría suceder
aún en la mismísima eternidad del pensamiento
que de pronto insista el dolor del pie ausente.

MIND UPLOADING

If one had built the technology needed to transfer
after scanning the microscopic layer of the brain
the mind to a technological or digital state
and achieve its freedom at last from bodily hindrance

it would be logical for that – what? I? – to give endless
time to pursuit of philosophical meditations
destined to reveal the benefits of putting aside
geometric reason's uncertainty and discordance:

that confused orb of multiple experiences
deriving from the always-fallible senses
of hearing or smell with their tendency to shake
the soul's reflections from the realm of extension.

But as for those who have lost to amputation
an arm or a leg, it is also possible
that in that self-same eternity of thinking
the missing foot would suddenly insist its ache.

PANAMAX

Ideado para capitalizar el máximo de espacio permitido
según las esclusas del reconocido canal, este carguero
capaz de alcanzar casi los trescientos metros de eslora
con una manga de más de treinta que ajusta ¡cuidado!
y la altura suficiente para pasar con marea alta o baja
calma y más de cuatro mil contenedores sobre cubierta
debajo del Puente de las Américas en Balboa, es historia.
También es historia la conformación estructural del canal
dado que hace días y en plebiscito nacional fue votada
(a riesgo de perder un porcentaje fundamental del PBI
según el gobierno, de aumentar la deuda según otros)
la ampliación necesaria para mantener la competitividad
y dar cabida al fin a los nuevos bulk-carrier adecuados
para transportar el triple y casi el cuádruple en cámaras
digitales y de video, juguetes, electrodomésticos, zapatos
e indumentaria de las más variadas y reconocidas marcas
que por el momento deben hacer un demorado, innecesario
y sobre todo costoso giro por el Cabo de Hornos tras partir
de Shenzhen o Shangai para llegar al puerto de Florida.
Es evidente que las tratativas que permitieron incorporar
la República Popular a la OMC están "moviendo las aguas"
y que hasta el marino más interesado de la tripulación
sólo verá, cuando se le señale con un gesto allá, allá
donde funcionara por décadas la School of the Americas
y los futuros graduados entrenaban en el conocimiento
del enemigo leyendo a Mao Tse-tung, un hotel * * * * *

PANAMAX

Built to maximise the space permitted to pass
the gates of that famous canal, this cargo ship
able to reach almost three hundred metres long
with a beam of more than thirty that fits – take care! –
and the correct height to pass at high tide or low
calm with more than four thousand containers on deck
by the Bridge of the Americas, is history.
History too the canal's structural makeup
as a few days ago a referendum approved
(risking loss of a key fraction of GDP
says the government, of rising debt say others)
the widening needed to stay competitive
and give room to the new bulk carriers able
to transport triple, almost four times digital
cameras, videos, toys, appliances, shoes
clothes of the most various and recognised brands
that for now make a detour, unnecessary
and above all costly round Cape Horn after leaving
from Shenzen or Shanghai towards Florida's port.
It's clear the negotiations for the entry
of China to the WTO are 'making waves'
and that even the most interested sailor
will only see, when it's pointed out, that there is,
where for decades the School of the Americas
instilled in its future graduates the knowledge
of the foe through reading Mao, a ***** hotel.

PLASMALEMA

Pero si la vida exige
un límite para existir
o sea una membrana
llamada bicapa lipídica
capaz de distinguir
o inclusive separar
lo que está adentro
de lo que está afuera

también parece exigir
que ese mismo límite
tal como se deduce
de estudios citológicos
hechos con microscopio
electrónico o nuclear
además de reflexiones
menos instrumentales

sea semipermeable
se adapte una y otra vez
más sólido más fluido
y permita incesante
con criterios selectivos
interacción y entrada
a través de sus moléculas
de iones masa energía.

PLASMALEMA

But if life insists on
a limit to existing
that's formed of a membrane
called the lipid bilayer
that's able to distinguish
or even to separate
that which is inside
from that which is outside

it also seems to demand
that that very limit
as is deduced from
cytological studies
done with a microscope
electronic or nuclear
alongside reflections
that are less instrumental

is semipermeable
can adapt time and again
more solid more fluid
and permits ceaselessly
with selective criteria
interaction and entrance
across its molecules
of ions mass energy.

QUIMANTÚ

En su período de diputado había presentado
un proyecto de ley para fundar una editorial
"en beneficio de las capas" (se lee en el parte
al congreso elevado) "modestas de la población"
así que cuando fue votado como presidente
ante la quiebra de una existente no lo dudó
y en los talleres y oficinas atiborradas técnicos
y profesionales movidos por el nuevo desafío
corrían de un lado al otro eligiendo tipografías
para colecciones literarias, para los cuadernos
de educación popular con el título Explotados
y explotadores y también cuentos infantiles
con un tiraje que podía alcanzar setenta mil
y una distribución hasta ese entonces inédita
en kioskos y estaciones que alcanzaba a cubrir
todo lo largo del territorio hasta Punta Arenas
utilizando bólidos disponibles de la Aviación.
Por eso después era intrincado para la Junta
diferenciar con sutileza un libro de un arma:
las imágenes de los soldados junto a las piras
en las que ardían ejemplares en una esquina
bajo el complejo de Remodelación San Borja
no podían sino leerse como una advertencia;
para evitar el problema de los malentendidos
prefectos en camiones allanaron la casa central
y, ya que estaban, bibliotecas populares varias

QUIMANTÚ

During his time as a deputy he had presented
a proposal for a new law to found a publisher
'for the benefit of the lower' (so reads the paper
delivered to Congress) 'sections of the population'
and consequently when he was elected as president
he didn't wait following a publisher's bankruptcy
and in the crowded offices and workshops the technicians
and professionals motivated by the new challenge
hurried from one side to another choosing typefaces
for literary collections, for the exercise books
for popular education with the title Exploited
and Exploiters and also for books written for children
which received a print run of up to seventy thousand
and a distribution that until then had been unheard
of in kiosks and stations that extended to cover
the whole length of the land as far as Punta Arenas
using fast vehicles the Air Force made available.
So afterwards it was intricate work for the Junta
to tell the subtle differences between a book and a weapon:
the images of the soldiers standing next to the pyres
where copies burned at San Borja Renovation Complex
could only be a warning; and to avoid misunderstandings
lorryloads of policemen ransacked the central office
and, as they were there, various popular libraries

y hasta el subsuelo de facultades infectadas.
¿Quién no querría, con ansias de sobrevivir,
en silencio quemar sus volúmenes en el patio?
Y sin embargo muchos tomitos aún aparecen
–e inclusive cada tanto seguirán emergiendo–
porque nunca falta quien temeroso y todo
guarde alguno tras las vigas del entretecho,
quien le arranque las páginas de la salutación
oficial a la antología nerudiana, cambie tapas,
entierre envuelto el suyo en cualquier galpón.

even down to the basements of infected faculties.
Who, anxious to survive, would not have made the decision
in silence to burn their volumes on the patio?
Nevertheless still today many little tomes still appear
and every now and then will still keep coming to light
because there's always someone who, daring and all,
keeps one behind beams in the attic, who tears out
the Neruda anthology's official frontispiece,
changes covers, buries their own in any old warehouse.

RECUEIL (DES PLANCHES)

¿Existe para un filósofo tarea más digna
que reflexionar con sistema del proceso
de manufactura de un par de medias?

Ya era hora de discutir la superioridad
supuesta de la música sobre la carpintería
la cordelería y, más vale, la peluquería:

¡cuánta inteligencia, método y saber
en el arte de ensombrecer el terciopelo
o de calibrar la juntura de dos maderas!

Para reunir ese conocimiento en un libro
hubo que levantar la vista del libro y salir
a visitar talleres, hacerle cien preguntas

al bonetero, rápido anotar sus términos
confusos a ser rectificados después
además de diseñar los grabados en cobre

donde se podía ver con precisión el dibujo
de cada herramienta (fig. 3 escofina)
la máquina para producir la trencilla

RECUEIL (DES PLANCHES)

Is there for a philosopher a higher task
than to reflect systematically on socks
and the processes used in their manufacture?

It was time already to discuss the supposed
higher nature of music over carpentry
ropemaking and, especially, wigmaking:

but how much intelligence, method and wisdom
in the art of shading the pile of new velvet
or measuring the joint of two pieces of wood!

To bring together all this knowledge in a book
required lifting his gaze from the book going out
to visit workshops, to ask a hundred questions

of the milliner, rapidly record his terms
incorrectly but to be tidied up later
and above all to design copper engravings

in which you could see with precision the drawings
of every piece of equipment (figure 3: a rasp)
the machine that is used for producing the braid

del vestido que el propio enciclopedista
utilizaba e inclusive el espacio de trabajo
en el que hombres y mujeres se movían ya

como si formaran parte del mecanismo
de uno de los relojes cuyo funcionamiento
aparecía también ilustrado en las láminas.

Pero cuando el sabio entusiasta entraba
a la factoría tal diafanidad no existía: olores
densos salían de ahí, los ruidos de la masa

hacían dificultosa la escucha, el encargado
desconfiaba en nombre del secreto gremial,
una polea como suele suceder se trababa

el más experto tartamudeaba, alguna risa
sonaba entre las pelucas, ¿Y este quién es?
se oía, en algún francés, atrás de la fragua.

covering the clothes that this same encyclopaedist
dressed in and also the places of employment
in which men and women were moving around now

as if they formed a part of the mechanism
built into one of the timepieces whose functioning
also appeared illustrated among the plates.

But when the enthusiastic sage went into
the factory that transparency did not exist: dense
smells drifted out of it, the noises of the mass

made it difficult to listen, the floor manager
was suspicious on behalf of the trade secret
a pulley got stuck as very often happens

the best expert kept stuttering, a laugh sounded
among the wigs, And who is this chap? could be heard
muttered in some kind of French there behind the forge.

SÄKERHETSKOPIERING

El frenesí de la comunicación fluida y de inmediato
transportada o al menos en milisegundos exige
memoria sin interrupción o sea barriles y barriles
de petróleo denso o toneladas de carbón extraído

de un modo menos fluido entre un polvillo espeso
apropiado para exhibir la transparencia imposible
de todo intercambio, de ahí que la compañía
oferente de los servicios de una red social digital

busque incrementar la eficiencia del uso energético
así como del orbe semántico de las connotaciones
construyendo con módulos de diseño tipo ikeano
en un claro de un bosque cercano al círculo ártico

enormes galpones donde las altísimas temperaturas
producidas por los cientos de miles de servidores
ubicados en estanterías interminables y vigiladas
por uno o dos técnicos montados sobre un scooter

se moderen gracias al aire frío propio de la región.
Toda rodeada de nieve y de pinos la construcción
permite ofrecer una imagen aséptica del proceso.
Eso, además de la proximidad a un río caudaloso

SÄKERHETSKOPIERING

Frenzy of fluid communication that's instantly
transported or at least is in milliseconds demands
unbroken memory or rather barrels and barrels
of dense petroleum or tonnes of coal excavated

in a much less fluid manner and in a thick dust cloud
suitable to show the impossible transparency
of any interchange, meaning that now the company
offering the services of a digital network

seeks to increment efficiency of energy use
alongside the semantic orb of associations
building in modules of Ikea-style design
in a clearing in the woods close to the Arctic Circle

enormous hangars where the elevated temperatures
emanating from the hundreds of thousands of servers
deposited on interminable shelves watched over
by one or two technicians travelling on a scooter

are moderated thanks to the cold air of the region.
The construction, completely surrounded by snow and pines,
permits to us an aseptic image of the process.
That, and the proximity of a free-flowing river

pautado por una docena de represas que regulan
mientras cae el agua desde lo alto en sus turbinas
su curso bajando el costo general de la electricidad
sumado a la estabilidad política de un país nórdico

estuvo en la base de la preferencia por este sitio
apto para indicar el carácter global de la empresa.
En los meses de invierno se puede caminar el mar.
Todo el movimiento se congela hasta el horizonte,

aunque el pescador lugareño que perfora un hueco
en el hielo y sentado sobre una silla sobre eskíes
espera tras lanzar con experiencia el anzuelo sabe
que una trucha camaleónica en el fondo se agita.

contained by a dozen dams erected to regulate
while the water falls from on high through their turbines
its flow shrinking the general cost of electricity
plus a Nordic country's political stability

was the basis for the preference for selecting this site
apt for showing the global character of the business.
In the winter months it's possible to walk on the sea.
All movement has been frozen as far as the horizon;

nevertheless the local fisherman who breaks a hole
in the pack ice and settles himself on a seat on skis
and waits after casting with experience his hook knows
that a chameleonic trout is moving deep below.

SINNLICH

Ah, no, no era solo un ánimo sentimental
exacerbado y pasajero capaz de escribir
una novelita sobre un ánimo sentimental
exacerbado y pasajero, era a la vez ése
capaz de descubrir el hueso intermaxilar
suavemente dibujar con grafito del granito
la dureza hasta captar su edad geológica
recordarle al mecanicista que los colores
premeditan además los temperamentos
o cotiledones brácteas sépalos estambres
hojas y pistilos comparar para ver así
una misma forma en dinámica continua…
Su vida fue la negación de la disociación.
Al entendimiento de la ciencia le faltaba
el entendimiento del arte, esa cosa física
de la experiencia directa. Horas de mirar
una piedra hasta poder intuir su historia.
Pero ya la más amada estaba prometida
y la comunidad de los físicos se burlaba.
La división del trabajo inauguraba el final
de una fantasía humanista y omnilateral.
¿Cómo explicar su curiosidad versátil?
Por el atraso del desarrollo de su nación.
La miseria a veces puede ser opulencia.

SINNLICH

Ah, no, he was not just a sentimental soul
exaggerated and flighty able to write
a novella about a sentimental soul
exaggerated and flighty, he was also
able to describe the intermaxilial
smoothly sketch out its hardness with graphite
even capturing its geological age
to remind the mechanic that colours
also premeditate temperaments
or compare cotyledons bracts sepals stamens
leaves pistils to see there an identical form
in continuous dynamism. His life was
the negation of all disassociation.
The understanding that science had was lacking
the understanding of art, that physical thing
of direct experience. Hours of gazing at
a stone until able to perceive its story.
But already the best beloved was engaged
and the physicist community was mocking.
The division of labour began the ending
of humanist, omnilateral fantasy.
How could one explain his versatile curiosity?
By the delayed development of his nation.
Sometimes misery can be opulence.

SKEP

¿Cuál es el problema de cualquier analogía?
Establecer la extensión de la semejanza.

Una antigua colmena de paja a mano tejida
apta para permitir la acumulación de miel

y de ideas dulces sobre el trabajo colectivo
se estampó por años en las notas de crédito

de uno de los cuatro bancos de Gran Bretaña
hasta ser sustituida por la figura de un caballo

azabache, noble, impetuoso por lanzarse
a la carrera y, obvio, ya de carácter individual.

El problema de tal sistema de la apicultura
previo a la invención de los panales móviles

era su faz arcaica, irracional y poco lucrativa;
no existía entonces otro modo de remover

la producción obtenida sin quemar azufre
para evitar con el humo alrededor las picadas

de quienes pretendían defender su labor
y luego con el instrumento de recolección

SKEP

What is the problem with any analogy?
To know the extent of the similarity.

An old-fashioned beehive made of straw hand woven
apt to permit accumulation of honey

And some sweet ideas about collective labour
was printed for many years on the credit notes

of one of the four greatest banks of Great Britain
until it was replaced by the form of a horse

black as jet, and eager to launch itself
into a run and, of course, individual.

The problem with the system of apiculture
before movable honeycombs were invented

was archaism, irrational, low-earning;
no other means then existed of removing

the product obtained than setting light to sulphur
to prevent with the smoke drifting around the stings

of the workers aiming to defend their labour
and then using the instrument of collection

destruir lamentablemente todas las celdas
a ser renovadas con una colonia nueva.

La conciencia sobre posibles interpretaciones
erróneas o excesivas debe haber justificado

la modificación tardía de este símbolo tomado
a su vez de los billetes de la entidad nacional

en los cuales por primera vez había aparecido
por su parecido a una pila áurea de monedas;

también tal vez para señalar con sofisticación
la función clave y suprema de la abeja reina.

lamentably make a ruin of all the cells
to be renovated with a new colony.

The awareness of the possible incorrect
or excessive readings must have then justified

the modification of this symbol taken
in turn from the notes of the national entity

upon which for the first time it had been printed
picked for its likeness to a golden pile of coins;

and perhaps to signal with sophistication
the vital and supreme function of the queen bee.

TRANSPORT COSTS

Más acá del lirismo de los reclamos
sobre el carácter disruptivo del arte

el poema también es un commodity
elaborado con un material específico

y por tanto hay que evaluar los costos
de ponerlo a circular en el mercado;

más particularmente de transportarlo;
esto es: de una lengua a otra lengua

de una más acotada en su alcance
a otra de hablantes más numerosos

de una literariamente empobrecida
a otra de capital ya consolidado

o también al revés entiéndase esto
en términos literales o figurados.

Ergo si estuviera leyendo estos versos
aunque no en su versión en español

le agradecería distinga a quien abrió
el diccionario para evaluar los matices

TRANSPORT COSTS

More than the lyricism of the claims
for the disruptive power of the art

the poem is too a commodity
made with a specific material

and so it's necessary to weigh up the costs
of circulating it in the market;

more particularly transporting it;
that is: from one language to another

from one that is limited in its reach
to one that has more numerous speakers

from an impoverished literature
to another with solid capital

or that's also in reverse understood
in literal or figurative terms.

And ergo if I were reading these lines
albeit not in their Spanish version

I'd thank you to point out he who opened
the dictionary to assess the exact

exactamente de estas mismas palabras
pensando quizá por qué habrá elegido

un trabajo no del todo bien pago
mientras su hijo lo llamaba para jugar.

nuances of this vocabulary
wondering perhaps why he settled on

an employment that's not very well paid
while his son called to him to come and play.

VALENÇAY

La identidad se paga. La tradición se paga.
Eso paga el Estado francés cuando subsidia
una actividad agrícola cuya mano de obra
en jornadas ya no más medidas por el alba
y el ocaso sobre unos terrenos roturados
desde al menos unos siete milenios atrás
rauda se reduce al igual que el porciento
de su participación real en el PBI. Un tiempo
paga. Un tiempo ancestral que solo existe
financiado por millones y más millones.
No paga la leche de una cabra alpina. No
paga las cenizas de carbón con que cubrir
la cuajada. No paga la habitación húmeda
y ventilada donde se lo dejará madurar.
Paga la persistencia de una idea, el paisaje
adecuado a esa idea. El orgullo nacional
paga, paga una frase de Brillat-Savarin.
(Se aconseja acompañarlo con un Shiraz.)

VALENÇAY

Paying for an identity. Paying for tradition.
The French state is paying for those when it subsidises
an agricultural activity whose labourers
in days that are no longer measured from dawn until dusk
on farmland ploughed over for at least seven thousand years
reduce in number in proportion to the percentage
of its contribution to GDP. It is paying
for time. That is, an ancestral time that exists only
because it is financed by millions and still more millions.
It doesn't pay for alpine goat's milk. Nor does it
pay for the coating of charcoal that is dusted
on the rind. Nor for the humid, ventilated
room it's left in to mature. It pays to maintain
an idea, the suitable landscape. And for national pride
it pays, it pays too for a phrase by Brillat-Savarin.
(They say it is best accompanied by a nice Shiraz.)

WANLLASQA

Ccompis Leona Amachi Rosada Clavel
Maru millku Puka simi Puka pampiña
Canchán Pillpintuy Maru piña Yungay.
Hay más de tres mil nombres para decir
y más de tres mil sabores en la lengua.
Debajo de los toldos el mercado concreto
extendido en la plaza en medio del valle
exhibe una variedad de formas y colores
que su acepción más abstracta reduce
por una opción omnipresente y blanca
con metas de multiplicación industrial.
Cuelga el cartel sobre cada pila armada
sobre cada una de las bolsas abiertas
traídas en camiones de las laderas altas
donde se protege de la rancha y el tizón
una memoria frágil contra lo unívoco.
En la mano conviene elegir una a una;
mirarle los ojos, palparla y comprobar
que sea lisa, esté firme, no aguachenta.
La mariva se dora: sirve para rellenarla.
La huayro es absorbente: funciona bien
en estofados jugosos y platos con salsa.
La peruanita ya sabe rica hervida con sal;
mejor si le agrega un poco de manteca.
La tarmeña va al horno. La huamantanga
se pela fácil. La sirina ofrece vitamina C.
Con la guinda gaspar se viven más años.

WANLLASQA

Ccompis Leona Amachi Rosada Clavel
Maru milku Puka simi Puka pampiña
Canchán Pillpintuy Maru piña Yungay.
There are more than three thousand names to say
more than three thousand flavours for the tongue.
Under the awnings the concrete market
spread out in the square down in the valley
exhibits a range of forms and colours
whose most abstract significance boils down
to an option white and omnipresent
with goals of industrial multiplication.
A sign hangs over each assembled heap
above each one of the opened-out sacks
carried in lorries from the high hillsides
where they protect from the mould and the blight
fragile memory against the univocal.
It's best to choose them one by one by hand;
look it in the eyes, squeeze it and ensure
it's smooth, it's firm and it's not watery.
The mariva turns gold: good for filling.
The huayro is absorbent: works well
in juicy stews and dishes with salsa.
The peruanita's tasty with salt;
better if you serve it with some butter.
The tarmeña cooks well in the oven.
The huamantanga peels easily.
The sirina offers vitamin C.
With the guinda gaspar you'll live more years.

WARISATA

A casi cuatro mil metros de altura sobre el mar
junto a las faldas nevadas de la cordillera ahí
de la superficie lacustre multiplicada en reflejos

no hace falta construir el edificio de una escuela
para iniciar el período escolar. El período escolar
se inicia con la construcción misma del edificio.

Primera lección entonces: fabricación de adobe.
¿Cómo se aprende? Fuera del aula, o levantando
mejor sus paredes con barro, paja, unos moldes.

¿Según qué criterios se organizan los programas?
De acuerdo a las necesidades de la vida comunal.
La clase se da en un taller, un huerto, ¡la llanura!

¿Y los horarios de la jornada? No hay. Si en la noche
nieva habrá que levantarse de la cama de totoras
para salir a cuidar almácigos de cebolla y coliflor.

Hoy teníamos aritmética pero... ¡floreció la quinua!
Vengan, vengan, vengan. Conversemos mejor
de naturales y enseñanza agrícola. ¿Qué saben?

Para la clase de historia se intentará volver a usar
el viejo acueducto inkaiko a fin de tener bajo riego
las hileras sociales de papa, oca, haba y papalisa.

WARISATA

Nearly four thousand metres above sea level
up beside the snowy slopes of the mountains there
and the lake surface multiplied in reflections

we have no need to construct a new school building
before beginning the term. The school term instead
gets started with the construction of the building.

So the first lesson: the making of adobe.
How do we learn? Outside the classroom, or raising
better its walls using mud, straw, some moulds.

By what criteria do we frame the programme?
In line with the daily needs of communal life.
We hold the class in a workshop, the garden, on the plain!

And the timetables? There are none. If in the night
it snows we have to get up from the bulrush beds
and tend the onion and cauliflower seedlings.

Today, arithmetic but … the quinua's in bloom!
Come quickly, come, come. It's much better if we talk
of nature and agrarian skills. What do you know?

In history class we are trying to restart
the Inca aqueduct so as to irrigate
social potato, oca, bean and papalisa rows.

Se produce conocimiento y sombreros a la vez,
alfombras tiwanacotas y polleras para ofrecer
en el mercado porque no hay vida sin economía.

Y para sostener el proyecto de producir maestros
también, rurales y bilingües: porque cada lengua
arma mundos diversos dentro de este mundo.

Pero los del Consejo Nacional de Educación vieron
anarquía en la currícula insólita y en la planificación
impertinente comunismo, peligro. Estaban en lo cierto.

We produce both knowledge and hats at the same time
and tiwanancota rugs and skirts for selling
in the market, as there's no life without economy.

And to sustain the aim of producing teachers
rural and also bilingual: because each tongue
creates many different worlds within this one world.

But the National Council for Education saw
anarchy in the strange syllabus, in the plans
insolent communism, danger. They were right.

WEIL BROTHERS

Una de las "cuatro grandes" compañías exportadoras
afincadas en la Argentina a fines del siglo diecinueve
éxtasis de la división internacional de la producción

Es decir: rápida expansión de la frontera agrícola local
siembra al voleo de maíz y variedad de trigo Barletta
en el aire una mano de las millones de manos arribadas

de la península itálica o ibérica con una memoria secular
de los ritmos fértiles de Ceres y las fiestas lupercalias
completamente inútil para estos suelos sin roca y casi

sin linde para arrendar mal y pagar con una cosecha
potencial ante el granizo y el retorno de la langosta
o de los braceros y crotos de todo tipo para la siega

el uso de la espigadora si se invirtió en capital parvas
más parvas parvas trilla y largo trecho a la estación
tras el embolsado obligado la estiba alta en el carro

y la pérdida de uno que otro cero ante la ignorancia
de los movimientos bruscos de ascenso y descenso
de los precios en pizarras del otro lado del mundo

WEIL BROTHERS

This was a business among the 'big four' exporting companies
based in Argentina at the end of the 19th century
ecstasy of the international division of production.

That is: rapid expansion of the local farming area
manually sowing seeds of maize and the Barletta strain of wheat
in the air one hand from among the millions of hands that arrived

from Italy or Iberia bringing ancient memories
of the fertile rhythms of Ceres and Lupercalian feasts
completely useless for these soils that are without rock and almost

without boundaries to rent badly and pay with a potential
harvest in the face of hailstorms and the return of the locust
or of the labourers and hobos of all kinds for the reaping

the use of the harvester if they invested capital grain
more grain grain threshing and hours of waiting around at the station
after the obligatory bagging heaped up high in the cart

and the loss of one zero or more resulting from ignorance
of the abrupt upward and downward movements of prices
written up on boards located on the other side of the world

cablegramas desde Londres o Rotterdam o Amberes
para distribuir la información a los agentes zonales de,
bueno, p. ej. esta empresa cuyas rentas financiaron

durante años los estudios de la Escuela de Frankfurt
dedicados a superar con elegancia la visión ortodoxa
economicista y mecanicista de base-superestructura.

cablegrams sent from London or Rotterdam or Antwerp
to distribute the information to the regional reps from,
well, for example this company whose income for many years

financially supported the research work of the Frankfurt School
devoted to elegantly overcoming the standard view
economic and mechanistic about base-superstructure.

XENOGAMY

Son varios los millones
de granos producidos
para que el viento
quizás quién sabe
alcance un estigma.

Adviértase la invención
del carácter esferoidal
destinado a sostenerse
el mayor tiempo posible
en el aire suspendido.

Es tal la preocupación
que aún en un pino
las piñas receptoras
y propagadoras están
unas arriba otras abajo

para evitar por gravedad
un encuentro indeseado.
A veces la estrategia
autoinventada consiste
en un desajuste temporal:

XENOGAMY

They're several these millions
of grains that are produced
in order that the wind
potentially who knows
brings one to a stamen.

Notice the invention
of the spheroid character
intended to sustain them
the longest possible time
suspended in the air.

So great is the concern
that even in a pine
the tree's receptor cones
and the propagators are
set some above some below

to avoid through gravity
an unwanted encounter.
Sometimes the self-devised
strategy consists in
temporal maladjustment:

o la hendidura se abre
antes de la maduración
polínica o las moléculas
ágiles son expulsadas
cuando no hay admisión.

La inversión en formas
aromas insinuantes y colores
para que sea convocado
el colibrí y en su pico
porte microgametofitos

buscando otro estigma
se ha producido a lo largo
de un tiempo lentísimo
que permite confirmar
las dosis de pérdidas

y creatividad requeridas
para evitar acudir así
a la solución más limitada
de todas: la reproducción
endogámica de lo mismo.

either the gap opens up
before the maturity
of the pollen or agile
molecules are expelled
when there is no entrance.

The investment in forms
seductive scents and colours
so that the hummingbird
is summoned which in its beak
carries microgametophytes

seeking other stamens
has arisen through the course
of the slowest of times
permitting confirmation
of the levels of losses

the creativity needed
so as to avoid turning
to the most limited means
of all: endogamic
reproduction of oneself.

悬挂

Dejemos de lado el carácter monumental de la obra
parte de la planificación destinada a transformar
usando un tercio del acero y la mitad del hormigón
que se produce a lo largo y a lo ancho del planeta
un paisaje milenario con infraestructura de avanzada;

testimonio concreto –en principio en sentido literal–
del crecimiento del PBI desde la apertura gradual
peculiar e incesante hacia la economía de mercado
y por tanto también demostración de la magnitud
omnipresente y proverbial de la instancia del Partido;

tampoco abordemos la relación entre la dimensión
colosal del proyecto y el tamaño igualmente colosal
de una reserva de mano de obra en movimiento
constante de las zonas rurales a las zonas urbanas
y cuya ocupación es garantía de conflictividad baja;

y ni siquiera pongamos a consideración la cuestión
más específica del desafío de ingeniería involucrado
en la edificación de este interminable puente colgante
capaz de superar en suspensión la corriente del Yangtsé
que parte el amplio territorio en dos amplias mitades

悬挂

Let's leave to one side the monumental nature
of the work, part of the plan designed to transform
using a third of the steel and half the concrete
that is produced the length and breadth of the planet
an ancient landscape through advanced infrastructure

concrete witness – chiefly in the literal sense –
to GDP growth since the gradual peculiar
incessant opening of the market economy
and therefore too a demonstration of the scale
omnipresent, proverbial of the Party's drive;

let's not think of the relation between the huge
dimensions of the scheme and equally huge size
of the reserve army of labour in constant
movement from rural areas to urban zones
and whose occupation guarantees low conflict;

let's not take into account the more specific
question of the engineering challenge involved
in building this interminable hanging bridge
overpassing in suspension the Yangtze's flow
that breaks the broad area into two broad halves

con el fin de sostener la autopista Pekín-Shanghai
mediante cables ultrarresistentes de gran espesor
hechos en realidad cada uno de miles y miles de cables
que parten de dos bloques de anclaje soterrados
en los suelos inundables de ambas puntas de la costa;

más bien reparemos en la cuadrilla sobre la pasarela
allá en lo más alto, venidos todos de una misma localidad
alejada a kilómetros según un método de contratación
pensado para privilegiar el uso de un dialecto común
necesario para entender indicaciones sin interferencias;

fijémonos entonces en ésos que acaban de terminar
de ajustar esos cables por lo pronto no tan tirantes
como sus propios nervios en una tarea de alto riesgo
dominando el vértigo de la altura y de la historia:
tal vez sean ellos la verdadera obra en construcción.

so as to bear the Beijing-Shanghai motorway
on ultra-resistant cables of great thickness
each really made from many thousands of cables
that stretch outward from two anchoring blocks buried
in the flood plains along each side of the river;

better we focus on the gang on the walkway
there at the highest point, all from one area
kilometres away via a contracting scheme
devised to privilege a common dialect
so as to understand instructions without confusion;

we will look also at those who have just finished
adjusting the cables suddenly not as tense
as their own nerves in a high-risk activity
overcoming height and history's vertigo;
perhaps they are the real work under construction.

ZAFRA

El concepto a plantear en la plenaria de Camagüey
era la relación dialéctica entre conciencia y trabajo.
Por eso antes del discurso se subió a la cortadora

y en unos días cortó cuarenta y cinco mil arrobas.
Ya era una declaración, al menos la base empírica
donde sostener unas cuarenta y cinco mil palabras.

El ministro veía en los macheteros a la vanguardia
de los pueblos oprimidos de Asia, África y América.
El machetero veía un cogollo, otro y después otro.

¿Cómo explicar que eso no era un cañaveral más
sino las reservas en potencia de las que dependía
la guerra contra la fuerza más grande de la historia?

Arriba sobre la máquina para revisar cómo funciona.
Mal. Lógico, si es nueva. Hay que saber por qué.
¡Son demasiadas cuchillas! Listo. Ahora otro tema.

La diferencia entre cortar para la empresa y cortar
para la revolución es que la revolución exige doble:
quiere un músculo con capacidad de abstracción.

ZAFRA

The theme to consider at the Camagüey conference
was the dialectic link between consciousness and work.
And therefore before his speech he mounted the harvester

and in a few days cut forty-five thousand *arrobas*.
This was a declaration, at least the factual base
that's able to support around forty-five thousand words.

The ministry saw in the *macheteros* the vanguard
for the oppressed of Asia, Africa and the Americas.
The *machetero* saw a cane, another, another.

How to get across that this was not just another field
but instead a potential reserve on which depended
the war against the most powerful force in history?

Up on top of the machine to look at how it's working.
Badly. Makes sense, as it's new. But we need to work out why.
There are too many blades! Fixed it. Now there is something else.

The difference in cutting for the company and cutting
for the revolution is, the revolution demands double:
it wants a muscle with capacity for abstraction.

Eso no es un surco, es la central, es purificación
y eficiencia en las calderas, divisas y tractor ruso,
diversificación e inminencia del mundo socialista.

Pero en la cooperativa las cuentas no daban bien.
Y aunque algunos se iban pensando cómo inventar
un reemplazo autóctono para los cardanes rotos

que por cuánto tiempo ya no se podrían comprar,
otros no entendían bien por qué trabajar tanto
para que llegue el día en que no se trabaje más.

No furrow this: it's a power plant, purification
and efficient boilers, it's cash and a Russian tractor,
diversification, the socialist world's imminence.

But in the cooperatives the numbers give no cheer.
And although a few would think about how to come up with
a domestic alternative for the broken coupling

that would not have been available for quite a long time
others didn't quite understand why there was so much work
to bring about the days in which you'd never work at all.

GLOSSARY

(Terms in order of appearance)

Poesía civil / Civil Poetry

Defense of Poetry a work considering the role of poetry and the poet by Percy Bysshe Shelley (1792–1822; see Introduction).

Pacific Railway Company a nineteenth-century, British-controlled railway (see Introduction).

Ode to a Nightingale a work by John Keats (1795–1821), considered one of the quintessential Romantic poems.

Sileno/Silenus a companion to Dionysus, the ancient Greek god of wine.

Puerto Galván a port of the city of Bahía Blanca.

Frondizi, Arturo (1908–1995) President of Argentina from 1958 to 1962.

Martínez de Hoz, José Alfredo (1925–2013) Argentine lawyer, statesman and economist; Minister of Economy from 1976–1981, during the civic-military dictatorship.

Gramsci, Antonio (1891–1937) Italian political theorist and philosopher, known for work on concepts such as 'hegemony' and the 'organic intellectual'.

Valéry, Paul (1871–1945) French poet and essayist. One of the symbolists, he ceased writing poetry in the late 1890s and dedicated himself to essays and a life-long intellectual diary, called the *Cahiers* [*Notebooks*].

Dante Alighieri (1265–1321) Italian poet, author of *The Divine Comedy*.

Brecht, Bertolt (1898–1956) German writer, philosopher and theatre practitioner.

Bashō, Matsuo (1644–1694) Japanese poet and master of the haiku (a short poem form, based on juxtapositions).

Para hacer una torta sin leche / To Make a Cake Without Milk This poem draws on a recipe used at the Museo del Puerto (see Introduction).

Royal a traditional brand of baking powder in Argentina.

Ciocchini, Héctor (1922–2005) Argentine poet, artist and critic (see Introduction).

Hypnerotomachia Poliphili – The Strife of Love in a Dream an influential early illustrated book credited to the Italian monk Francesco Colonna (1433–1527), published in 1499 in Venice by Aldus Manutius.

Lexikón / Lexikon

अनियमितता (aniyamitata, Hindi) irregularity.

Der Autor Als Produszent [The Author as Producer, German] title of a 1934 speech by German Marxist philosopher Walter Benjamin (1892–1940).

Tretiakov, Sergey (1892–1937) a Soviet writer and journalist.

Kolhoz (Russian) form of collective farm in the Soviet Union.

标签 (biāoqiān, Mandarin) label, tag.

Blake, William (1757–1827) English poet, artist and print maker particularly interested in the power of visionary and prophetic imagination.

CESO Centro de Estudios Socio-Económicos, a Chilean university sociology research institute opened in 1965 and closed after the coup led by General Augusto Pinochet in 1973.

Cuadernos del Centro de Estudios Socio-Económicos *Journal of the Centre of Socio-Economic Studies.*

Heraud, Javier (1942–1963) Peruvian poet and member of the Marxist Army of National Liberation, killed while attempting to launch an insurgency.

Turner, J. M. W. (1775–1851) English painter particularly known for his mastery of light effects.

Fortabat, Alfredo (1894–1976) Argentine businessman and industrialist; his heir was María Amalia Lacroze de Fortabat (1921–2012), his widow, known as 'La dama del cemento' (see Introduction).

Bishop of Hippo (354–430) St Augustine; his works include *The City of God*.

Thyssenkrupp German industrial conglomerate (see Introduction).

Foucault, Michel (1926–1984) French philosopher known for his investigations of power, discipline, madness and sexuality (see Introduction).

Glomeromycetes a type of fungus that lives interdependently with plant roots.

Ordovician a geological period covering 488 to 433 million years ago.

Gold Exchange Standard a quasi-global economic arrangement that tied currencies to the value of gold. It lasted in varying forms from the mid-nineteenth to the mid-twentieth centuries.

灰色气体 (huīsè qìtǐ, Mandarin) marsh gas (a potentially dangerous mix of methane and other gases, and a common hazard in mining).

Hadesarchaea a kingdom of single-celled organisms living deep underground or beneath the sea.

Inngeris (Malay) English (the administrative language of Singapore); Lee Kuan Yew (1923–2015) is often referred to as the founder of modern Singapore.

La Internacional (Spanish) *The Internationale*, socialist anthem, lyrics written by Eugène Pottier in 1871.

Ombú (Spanish) ombu tree, *phytolacca dioica*, a very large evergreen tree commonly found on – and nearly synonymous with – the Argentine pampas.

IPA India pale ale, which was brewed in Britain to a higher alcohol content than ordinary ale, so that it could be transported by ship to Anglo-Indian colonists in the late nineteenth and first half of the twentieth centuries without spoiling, and due to its greater flavour now popular among craft brewers.

ITO indium tin oxide, a material used in touch screens.

Keplerbahn (German) Kepler orbit, the movement of one celestial body in relation to another, named after the German astronomer Johannes Kepler (1571–1630).

Keywords title of a work of cultural studies by the Welsh author Raymond Williams (1921–1988).

ເຂົ້າ (khao, Lao) a type of rice.

Лацис, Анна (Russian) Anna Lacis (1891–1979), Russian actor, educator and theatre practitioner, an important influence on the work of Walter Benjamin (see note to 'Autor (Als Produzent, Der)', above).

Lavoro domestico (Italian) domestic labour; the poem refers to an edition of Karl Marx's *Capital*.

ЛК-110Я (LK-110I, Russian) a type of icebreaker ship.

Lukács, György (1885–1971) Hungarian philosopher and literary critic, author of influential studies of the novel and historical fiction (see Introduction).

ΝΆΡΘΗΞ, or νάρθηξ (narthex, Ancient Greek) a plant, in Greek mythology used by Prometheus to steal fire from the gods.

Titans in Greek mythology, the gods who ruled before the triumph of the Olympians.

The School of the Americas US-run military school in Panama (see Introduction).

Plasmalemma a plasma membrane.

Quimantú Chilean publishing house created by the socialist government of President Salvador Allende (the "he" in the opening line) in 1971.

Recueil (des Planches) (French) set of plates, a reference to the Enlightenment *Encyclopaedie* compiled by Denis Diderot (1713–1784) *et al*.

Säkerhetskopiering (Swedish) back up (of computers, mobile phones, etc.).

Sinnlich (German) sensual, sensuous; a reference to the German author and philosopher Johann Wolfgang von Goethe (1749–1832).

Skep (English) an early form of beehive.

Valençay a type of French cheese.

Brillat-Savarin, Jean Anthelme (1755–1826) French writer and pioneer of gastronomic writing famed for his work of 1825, *The Physiology of Taste*.

Wanllaqsa (Quechua) chosen, selected; the Quechua terms that follow are all words for varieties of potato.

Warisata a town and a school in Bolivia, known for its indigenous-centred education.

Weil Brothers German-Argentine export company (see Introduction).

Barletta southern Italian city, known for its wheat.

Xenogamy fertilisation by a genetically different member of the species (i.e. sexual reproduction).

悬挂 (xuán guà, Mandarin) suspension.

Zafra (Spanish) harvest; the poem refers to a speech given by the Argentine writer and revolutionary Ernesto 'Che' Guevara (1928–1967) at Camagüey, Cuba, in 1960 (see Introduction).

Arroba (Spanish) traditional measure in Hispanophone countries (see Introduction).

Machetero (Spanish) one who cuts crops with a machete.

www.ingramcontent.com/pod-product-compliance
Lightning Source LLC
Chambersburg PA
CBHW072008080825
30823CB00039B/2111